ROW[...]

She found h[...]
that had happen[...]
out to be," she [...]
telephone him! [...] ...I'll feel guilty because it
wasn't his fault you attacked him. Or yours, either, I
suppose. If anyone's to blame, I am. I know it isn't
smart to daydream on the street, but I wasn't
prepared to be accosted by a good-looking man.
Good-looking men lead to trouble. You did right to
bite him. I'm only sorry he took a misguided liking
to you."

She signed. "Oh well, you made the impression,
not me."

Dear Reader:

SILHOUETTE DESIRE is an exciting new line of contemporary romances from Silhouette Books. During the past year, many Silhouette readers have written in telling us what other types of stories they'd like to read from Silhouette, and we've kept these comments and suggestions in mind in developing SILHOUETTE DESIRE.

DESIREs feature all of the elements you like to see in a romance, plus a more sensual, provocative story. So if you want to experience all the excitement, passion and joy of falling in love, then SILHOUETTE DESIRE is for you.

For more details write to:

Jane Nicholls
Silhouette Books
PO Box 236
Thornton Road
Croydon
Surrey CR9 3RU

ELIZABETH ALDEN
No Sense of Humor

Silhouette Desire

**Originally Published by Silhouette Books
division of
Harlequin Enterprises Ltd.**

First published in Great Britain 1986 by Silhouette Books, 15–16 Brook's Mews, London W1A 1DR

© Elizabeth Alden 1985

Silhouette, Silhouette Desire and Colophon are Trade Marks of Harlequin Enterprises B.V.

ISBN 0 373 05225 1

22–0186

Made and printed in Great Britain by Richard Clay (The Chaucer Press) Ltd, Bungay, Suffolk

ELIZABETH ALDEN

is a current Arizona resident who has lived in several other states, England and Holland. A dedicated author, she writes children's books under another name and, in her spare time, hikes and goes bird-watching.

*For further information about
Silhouette Books please write to:*

Jane Nicholls
Silhouette Books
PO Box 236
Thornton Road
Croydon
Surrey CR9 3RU

1

The raw February wind from the East River struck Dave Archer's square jaw like a slap as his long legs ate up the blocks. With the dropping of the sun behind the tall buildings, Manhattan's slushy sidewalks were becoming icy. He had delivered his latest batch of cartoons to his editor and was on his way home to a blank drawing board and an empty store of ideas. But something amusing would undoubtedly occur to give him a push in the right direction.

Striding briskly, head up, he began to whistle. It was good to be in New York City and to have arrived at success as a cartoonist. He was healthy, in reasonably good shape financially and physically, and the fact that Karen had gone off and married a boatyard owner in Connecticut had ceased to bother him. He was well out of that complication.

His thoughts turned inward, he failed to notice the admiring looks cast his way by well-dressed women homeward bound at the end of the day. He still thought of himself as a country boy from Missouri, and he liked to dress the part—thick-soled Frye boots, blue jeans, sheepskin coat and muffler. The wind tossed his wavy brown hair and brought a glow to his cheeks and a sparkle to his blue eyes.

A few blocks from his destination his gaze fell on a dog. White, shorthaired and low-slung, it had a long ungainly head, sharp ears and small pink eyes. The very sight of it put Dave in high good humor. It was sniffing at the base of a storefront. A smallish woman in a puffy down coat held the dog's leash, her attention apparently focused on the delicatessen food in the window.

Dave halted beside her with a laugh.

"What breed is he?"

Jarred out of her reverie, the young woman flung Dave a startled look and stepped back to increase the space between them. Her heel encountered a spot of newly formed ice and she slipped. Dave caught her arm.

"Careful!" she cried. "Don't touch me!"

Dave goggled at her. Then from the corner of his eye he saw the dog whirl with a snarl and launch itself at his legs. He tore his attention from the wide brown eyes in the woman's startlingly beautiful face in time to see the animal sink its teeth into his booted ankle.

"Vicky!" the young woman screeched. "No! Bad dog!" She stared at Dave, her eyes appalled. "Why did you have to grab me?"

The animal growled. Dave's keen sight noted the way she braced her paws, every toe separated.

"Should I have stood by and let you fall?" he demanded.

"Yes! I mean—" She backed away a step, frowning. "What a dumb thing to do—come up behind me and scare me like that."

Dave stood calmly, not trying to remove his leg from the dog's grip. He was more interested in the animal's sturdy, ridiculous shape. It still made him want to laugh.

"How long before she lets go?" he inquired.

"You don't understand!" Vicky's owner cried, tugging without result at the dog's leash. "She's a bullterrier. She's still—a puppy. Vicky!" She dropped to her knees and tried without success to pull Dave's leg out of the dog's jaws. Then she looked up and scolded, "Don't you know better than to come up behind people with dogs and ask stupid questions?"

"I guess not." Dave grinned down into her distraught face. Beautiful, but too thin. "Take it easy. Vicky's only got her teeth in my boot. I don't feel a thing."

"You don't understand!" she repeated. She got to her feet and fastened both hands in the dog's collar and tugged. The dog kept her jaws gripped. The woman pulled at the dog, the dog held on, and Dave had to take a quick sidestep to keep his balance. At that she gave up and faced him belligerently.

"All right, now you know. Once a bullterrier sinks its teeth into an enemy, it holds on until the enemy is dead."

"If that means me, she's going to have a long wait."

"She made a misjudgment! You must have a dog, and she smelled it." The woman tugged again at the leash.

The dog looked blissfully unaware, her feet planted on the sidewalk, her little eyes glazed in some existential dream. The young woman was too scrawny, Dave decided. Had it not been for her dog, he never would have noticed her.

"I have a coon hound," he admitted.

"Then how could you be so stupid as to grab me?" she moaned, wringing her hands. "If someone grabbed you, wouldn't your dog protect you?"

Dave laughed. "He's too lazy to do anything so strenuous."

The woman responded with another moan. She seemed to have no idea what to do next. Two boys with skateboards stopped to watch and were joined by an old man. More onlookers would soon collect. Despite her belligerence, the young woman didn't look like she could handle that. In fact, she was so pale that Dave wondered if she was going to faint. Perhaps it was merely fright.

"Has your dog done this before?" he demanded.

"Once," she admitted, her eyes bright with angry embarrassment. "A deliveryman came in without knocking."

"What did you do then?" Dave asked with what he considered masterly patience.

"We fed her a hamburger."

"That's easy. I passed a restaurant back on that corner."

"I'll get one and come right back." She thrust the leash at Dave.

"Oh, no!" he cried before she could scurry off. He wasn't going to stand there looking like a fool until a hamburger could be produced. "We'll all go. I could use a cup of coffee. Will she let me move?"

"I don't know. . . ." The worried frown on the thin face told Dave that she wasn't as tough as she had first appeared.

"Let's find out. Maybe she's realized her mistake."

In response to Dave's good-tempered acceptance of the situation, the woman was abandoning her half-guilty, half-accusing attitude, but the bullterrier showed the tenacity of her kind, though she must have guessed by now that her zeal was misdirected. When Dave tried to take a step, she braced her legs and hung on.

"Vicky, you stupid thing, please let go!" the woman gritted. "Can't you see this man is friendly?"

Vicky's determined stance slowly eased. When Dave took a step, she growled but moved with him. Her teeth still inexorably clamped on his leg, she allowed herself to be dragged along the sidewalk.

Rowen Hill's only ambition at that moment was to disappear. She was strongly tempted to drop Vicky's leash and run. Never, she promised herself, would she take Vicky anywhere again without a muzzle, though what protection a muzzled dog would be she couldn't work out.

The man beside her chuckled, and she glanced up at him in amazement. From the beginning she had been aware of his good looks. The almost electric charge she had felt when he caught her arm had thrown her into such confusion that it was no wonder Vicky had sensed her panic and attacked him. He was not only handsome, he glowed with vitality and good humor.

"I like this dog!" he said, explaining his laughter. "She has a sense of the ridiculous. I suppose I should feel flattered that she only fastened her teeth in my boot and not in me."

"I never dreamed she'd attack anybody on the street," Rowen said, trying to apologize. "She's really rather sweet."

"Well, I did grab you. She was doing her duty. A bit overzealously, but still . . ." Dave glanced down at the animal. They were proceeding awkwardly along the sidewalk, the dog moving crabwise, taking every step with reluctance. The situation had the makings of a cartoon. Dave knew he would be able to come up with something funny.

"Vicky . . ." The young woman stooped to tug again at the dog's collar with a small white hand.

Dave noticed that she wore no rings and no gloves. She should be wearing gloves in this weather, he thought.

They reached the restaurant, luckily one that served hamburgers.

"At least we got the dog in," Dave commented under his breath as they reached an inconspicuous table near the door. "Why don't you go place our order? If the waitress sees Vicky, we'll all get kicked out."

Rowen hurried to the service bar to request the hamburger. After a minute she returned carrying mugs of steaming coffee.

"I hope a hamburger will do the trick," Dave said. Vicky sat at his feet, her jaws still clamped, her expression philosophical.

"Oh, I hope so, too!" Rowen looked so troubled that Dave was moved to try to put her at ease.

"If not, maybe she'll grow attached to me," he said, laughter in his voice. "My name's Dave Archer. What's yours?"

"Rowen Hill."

"Do you live around here?" She was older than he had thought at first, perhaps in her late twenties.

"Yes." She made an exclamation of annoyance. "I should have ordered the hamburger rare. It wouldn't have taken so long."

"Relax." Dave sipped his coffee. "The situation is under

control—unless they want to kick the dog out." He took a satisfying swig of his coffee and smiled at her. "I'm a cartoonist. If Vicky ever lets go of my leg, I'd like to draw her sometime."

Rowen's surprised eyes flew to his face. "You want to draw her?" she echoed.

"Yes. Do you think she and I could become friends? Or will she go for me again next time?"

She frowned. "She's really very sweet-tempered. But when a stranger comes up and grabs her mistress, what do you expect?"

"Okay, okay!" Dave raised both hands in capitulation. "Would you bring her to my studio some evening?"

"Uh, I suppose I could." Her eyes shifted. He could see she was wondering if his request was some crazy come-on.

"Vicky really owes me a favor," he reminded gently.

"Of course!" Rowen pulled herself together. "I just didn't think you'd ever want to see her again."

Dave grinned. "I've drawn my hound so often I could do it with my eyes closed. A new model might inspire me."

When she didn't reply but merely sipped her coffee in silence, Dave said, "So tell me about yourself."

"There's nothing to tell." Her dark lashes fanned her pale cheeks. She really was quite lovely in a reserved way, Dave thought.

"Where did you get this mutt?" he prodded.

"I bought her after some toughs came into my store—the store where I work. It's a small shop. Sometimes I'm the only one there. But—" She permitted a small smile to quirk the corner of her serious but beautiful mouth.

"But what?"

"But I didn't expect her to sink her teeth into strangers on the street."

Dave shrug dismissively. "What does your shop sell?"

"Rare books."

"Rare books . . ." Dave was delighted with the picture that came to him: this small lovely woman perched on a stool surrounded by shelves of leather-covered volumes, looking like a character out of Dickens, the white dog at her feet. He recognized the association. "Bill Sikes's dog was a bullterrier, wasn't he? In the movie."

"The movie *Oliver Twist?* That's right."

The hamburger arrived. The waitress who brought it looked at Dave with typical New York boredom.

"You can't have that dog in here," she stated.

"If she's not here, I can't be here," Dave pointed out. "She's attached to my leg."

"So take your leg out. The dog's gotta go." She laid the bill on the table.

Dave shrugged and fished for his wallet. Rowen was trying to explain to the waitress the purpose of the hamburger, but when she saw Dave's money she protested and pushed it away. Taking out her own billfold, she quickly settled the check, including a tip that made the waitress say, "Sorry, honey, but if a health inspector came in—" She raised her eyebrows and drew a finger across her throat. "You can take the plate if you bring it back when you're through."

Outside the restaurant, Rowen waved the patty in the air to cool it. Dave's stomach growled. The aroma made him wish he'd ordered one for himself. Rowen Hill looked like she could do with one, too.

"If Vicky won't eat it, we'll share it," he said. "You could use it."

Rowen shot him a dirty look, then crouched and waved the plate beside Vicky's nose.

"Here, sweetheart," she encouraged. The small eyes rolled toward the meat. Slowly, reluctantly, Vicky released her hold. Snuffling excitedly, she turned her attention to the plate. She wolfed down the patty almost before Dave could bend down to examine his pant leg.

"Do I run for it now?" he demanded.

"No, no! She'll be all right." To make sure, Rowen fastened her fingers in Vicky's collar. "Did she make a hole?" she asked anxiously, seeing Dave fingering his blue jeans.

"Slightly chewed and wet, that's all," Dave assured her.

"Listen, I meant that about sketching her." He fished in his pocket. "Here's my business card. Will you call me?" He felt an urge to walk her home, find out where she lived, talk to her longer. "I live on Sixty-seventh Street," he heard himself say. "I assume you live around here?"

She nodded toward the river. "Around the corner."

Dave kept a cautious eye on the dog, but Vicky seemed to accept her mistress's changed attitude. She stood placidly licking her chops, her ungainly head turning as she watched another dog walk by.

"You'll call?" Dave pressed.

Rowen said yes, but without enthusiasm. Dave wasn't used to cool responses. He could hardly help being aware that personable unattached men of his age were at a premium. Her manner awoke a spark of determination to pursue her acquaintance—because of the dog.

"Why don't you give me your phone number, in case you lose the card?" he urged.

"I'll call, I promise. Thank you for taking everything so well."

"I feel flattered that she liked me enough to hang on."

Rowen smiled at that and turned away. Dave stood and watched them go.

Striding home, he felt oddly elated. Rowen—a different name, and a woman so different from Karen that his mind quickly dismissed her, although he hoped she would call. If she didn't, he could stroll back this way with Clancy, his hound, and sooner or later they'd meet. People who owned dogs had to walk them. This strategy wasn't because he wanted to see her again, though—she was too thin and scrawny, and yet . . . He felt a sensation he could describe only as protective. He didn't know why she struck him as needing protection. Her fur-lined boots and down coat looked warm and expensive. What then—her lack of gloves? He tried to shrug away the thought. With Karen out of his hair, he didn't intend to protect anyone except himself, his dog, his cat and his career. Rowen had stood up for herself well enough.

He almost laughed at the way she had tried to blame him for

Vicky's misconduct. Maybe that would work into a joke—a huge dog snarling at a man's leg and its female owner saying, "She's insulted when you call her 'Nice girl.'"

By the time he reached home his good humor had returned.

Rowen was seething. She found herself blaming the dog for everything that had happened.

"Some protection you turned out to be," she stormed. "Now I'm obliged to telephone him! If I don't, I'll feel guilty, because it wasn't his fault you attacked him. Or yours, either, I suppose. If anyone's to blame, I am. I know it's not smart to daydream on the street. I was wondering if that volume of Thoreau might turn out to be valuable. I just wasn't prepared to be accosted by a good-looking man. Good-looking men lead to trouble, Vicky. You did right to bite him. I'm only sorry he took a misguided liking to you." She sighed. "Oh, well, you made the impression, not me. He wouldn't have given me a second thought. I could tell. So if I do take you to his studio, he'll do some sketches or take some photographs and your debt will be paid. Period."

Resentfully she tried to smother a wisp of regret. He *had* been exceptionally attractive. She liked his rangy build and the laughter lurking in his eyes. Disturbed by the flutter she felt at the thought of seeing him again, she reminded herself that her emotions were capped and were going to stay capped for a long safe time. Hadn't she had enough of charming men?

She turned the corner onto secluded, reserved Sutton Place, its gray facades and bare trees clean and elegant, then let herself into a house in the middle of the block.

"Celia!" she called from the entryway. "Are you home?"

"In here." The answer came from the living room, where a fire burned brightly in a white marble fireplace. Celia, wearing a black velvet jumpsuit, lay stretched on the couch, reading.

Rowen unfastened Vicky's leash and removed her own coat before joining her friend.

"Aren't you going out?" she asked in amazement.

"Hal is stuck at the office, and Roberto is out of town."

"I hope you told Pearl you'd be eating in."

"I did."

Noting that Celia already had a drink, Rowen crossed to the small bar and poured herself a glass of Dubonnet. She settled in a chair near the fire. Vicky stretched out at her feet, and Rowen prodded the dog with a firm toe.

"You shameless flirt! You've gotten me in trouble."

Celia regarded Rowen with interest. "What's she done?"

Rowen shook her head, suppressing a laugh. "Some idiot walked up behind me on First Avenue and surprised me, and made me slip. It's icy out. He grabbed my arm to keep me from falling. Vicky thought I was being attacked and grabbed his ankle."

"She bit him?"

"He was wearing boots, thank heaven, but she set her jaws and wouldn't let go."

Celia's eyes widened. "What did you do?"

"Dragged her to a restaurant and fed her a hamburger."

"The man dragged her?"

"Yes, actually." Rowen took a sip of her wine.

"He must have liked that. What happened then?"

"Actually, he seems to have fallen in love with her."

"Not you?"

"No." Rowen made a bitter grimace. "He couldn't tell I'm a gold mine just by looking."

"Stop that!" Celia commanded. "He might have liked you for yourself."

"Well, he didn't." Rowen realized she sounded sulky. She added quickly, "Not that I wanted him to."

"What did he look like?" Celia demanded. "Eligible?"

"He looked all right. Light brown hair . . . big . . . good-looking."

"How old?"

"Thirty-five, thirty-six."

Celia rolled her eyes. "Vicky has good taste."

Rowen denied it. "The guy's nuts. He's a cartoonist and he wants to draw her. He made me promise to bring her to his studio."

Celia grinned. "I thought you were through with men."

"I am! But what could I do? Vicky *did* attack him. He could have made all kinds of trouble, but he was nice. Letting him sketch her is the least I can do. He doesn't have to find out anything about me."

"If he knows you have a Sutton Place address, he doesn't need to know any more except that you're single."

"I didn't tell him where I live. He gave me his card." She went to her coat pocket and returned with it. "Dave Archer," she read. "Commercial artist."

"Nice name," Celia commented.

"Commercial artist," Rowen repeated. "He told me he draws cartoons!"

"He probably does both. There can't be much of a living in cartoons."

Rowen's eyes narrowed. "I think I'll tell him I'm house-sitting this place if something comes up about where I live."

"Why would you do that?"

"Oh, I don't know. . . ." Rowen swung her booted leg over the chair arm, her gaze abstracted. "I'd like to see how I'd be treated if . . ."

"If what?"

"If someone I met didn't know my family left me a lot of money."

Celia stiffened. "Do you think I treat you all right?"

"Of course, silly!" Rowen exclaimed, her wide brown eyes fastening on her friend's suddenly flushed countenance. "I meant men."

"Oh." Celia looked a little guilty. "You never told me you wanted your circumstances kept secret."

"I only just thought of the idea." Rowen's smile was impish. "Anyway, the men you've introduced me to expect a friend of yours to have a few bucks or we never would have met. But this man . . . If he liked me, I'd know it was for myself."

"Aha! So he did stir something in your heart."

Rowen smiled at her friend's expression and then gazed at the fire. "I'm not sure. Anyway, it might be a kick. Maybe he

17

won't even ask where I live, though he seems to be the nosy type." She scowled at the memory of his casual demand that she tell him about herself. Did he think she related her life story to every person she met by chance?

"Maybe he won't want to see Vicky more than once," she said, attempting to put his laughing blue eyes out of her mind.

"What if he does think you're poor?" Celia asked curiously.

"Not poor. Just a working person, like he is."

"That's poor in my book. Anyway, what difference will it make?"

"I don't know. . . ." Rowen's eyes slid back to the fire. "All kinds of things might be different. I might be different. Joe once said I was arrogant."

"You, arrogant?" Celia laughed.

"You don't know how I am with men. I know I'm independent. I've never tried hard to please any of them. Deep down inside, I guess I figured if they got me they were getting a pretty good package. That works all right until you're married and you're close to someone day in and day out." Her eyes saddened. "It takes two people to make a marriage fail, Celia."

"Not if one of them is Joseph Skeffington the Third," Celia countered loyally.

Rowen smiled at her friend. "Anyway, I'm going to pretend to be somebody else for a while. So if I ever bring home a handsome man with laughing eyes, don't forget I'm the house sitter."

"Well, you *are* house-sitting," Celia pointed out. "We both are. Your aunt and uncle are in Europe; that makes us house sitters. This guy doesn't have to know you could buy a place like this." Celia studied her friend. "You look like a waif."

"Stop it! I'm a thirty-year-old divorcée."

Celia raised one shoulder. "Where does he live?"

"The card says Sixty-seventh Street."

"Well, if you go, you'll have Vicky for protection."

"He didn't look dangerous," Rowen said.

"Well, he sounds different. I've tried to interest you in a

stockbroker"—Celia counted on her fingers—"two lawyers and a Coast Guard lieutenant, all to no avail."

"And the fact that I'm skinny didn't bother them a bit."

"Why should it? That's easily changed, and you're still pretty." Celia patted her flat stomach. "Speaking of weight, what time is dinner?"

"I'm not surprised you don't know. You're always eating out."

"You could be, too, if you'd stop torturing yourself for making a mistake. Who isn't divorced these days?"

"I don't mind being divorced"—Rowen's eyes flashed—"but I do mind the way he took me for everything. Other women aren't such fools, as the trustees remind me every time they see me."

"Men aren't all like that," Celia protested.

"Yes, they are!"

Celia laughed. "You'll change your mind sooner or later."

Rowen shook her head. In a sudden shift of mood she tore Dave Archer's card in two and threw it into the fire.

2

At the end of a week Dave realized with indignation that she wasn't going to call. During the last few days he had responded to a call for help from the advertising agency where he sometimes worked. They were desperate, because half the art department had the flu. But he had been home every evening.

"Clancy"—he addressed the coon hound—"are we going to let that animal get away with biting me?" He stacked his dinner dishes in the sink and reached for his coat. "I'm going to parade you up and down that street every night for a month, if necessary. I can't rest until I draw that mutt. I see her in my dreams." He wouldn't admit, even to himself, that sometimes he saw Rowen's thin, beautiful face, too.

The first four nights he had no luck, though he tried varying hours from early evening to late. He told himself there must be other bullterriers he could draw, but in patrolling the area where he had met Rowen and Vicky he saw none.

"Although we've met every other breed in existence," he teased his hound.

By the fifth night he was wondering if Rowen really lived in

NO SENSE OF HUMOR

the area. Perhaps he was being a mite fixated. New York City was full of amusing dogs.

But when he saw Rowen ahead of him later that same evening, he forgot his annoyance. His heart leapt with the satisfaction of success. Actually, he saw Vicky's gleaming white shape first. Not many pedestrians were about, it being close to nine o'clock.

He approached with caution, keeping Clancy and himself close to the curb as he came abreast of Rowen.

"Well, well, well!" he said with hearty surprise. "Fancy meeting you again."

"Oh, hi." Rowen had the grace to look ashamed.

"I believed you when you promised to call," Dave said, pretending to feel disillusion.

"I. . . ." It was on the tip of her tongue to say she had lost his card, but she found she couldn't lie under his direct blue gaze. "I didn't think you really meant it," she mumbled.

Both parties kept a wary eye on their dogs. The animals exchanged sniffs.

"I *did* mean it," Dave said, wondering why he had gone to the trouble of tracking her down. He couldn't force her to come to his studio.

"All right." Rowen took a deep breath and capitulated to fate. "How about tomorrow night?"

"Do you mean that?"

"If it's a good time for you."

"Any evening is fine."

"Tomorrow, then."

Dave drew a pleased breath and felt generous. "If you care to come after work, I'll cook something." She still looked like she needed a good meal. "Vicky can get used to the place while we eat."

Rowen nodded and wondered what she was letting herself in for.

"How is she with cats?" he questioned.

"No problem. I have—there are two at the house," she corrected herself.

"Great! I'll see you tomorrow then." Dave turned to leave before she changed her mind.

"Wait! What's your address? I'm afraid I mislaid your card," she admitted.

"Mislaid in the wastebasket?"

"Something like that." She gave a rueful smile.

He pretended to search his pockets for another card, brought it out and then repeated his address, to drive the point home.

"I'll be there—I really will," she told him.

Dave believed her. Nevertheless, on the way home he planned his menu around *boeuf bourguignon*. If she changed her mind again, he'd eat it two days in a row.

Walking Vicky to work the following morning, Rowen knew she would keep the appointment. She couldn't break her word twice. Normally she was honest and dependable. Proof of this was that she regularly opened the shop at the stated hour of nine-thirty, although her partner, Horace Rosenblum, seldom arrived until afternoon and would not have reproved her for shortening the morning hours.

How thankful she was to have the shop to go to! She had seen it as a lifeline that day when she had dropped in to say hello. She had known portly white-haired Mr. Rosenblum all her life. He had been a friend of her grandfather's, who had been an avid collector of journals of exploration. The previous spring, when Horace had told her that he was giving up his shop, she had been shaken out of her own misery.

"Giving it up?" she had exclaimed.

Horace had nodded unwillingly. "I'm not as energetic as I once was. I don't get to enough auctions to keep up the stock, and the rent is being raised again."

Rowen had glanced involuntarily at the overflowing shelves.

"Yes, yes, you see books from floor to ceiling. Bookshops must look crowded, but much of it is filler and should go out on sale tables." He shrugged. "This business has been my life. My nephews, their sons, nobody is interested in beautiful books. Now all is paperback."

"I'm interested," Rowen had insisted. "I kept Grandpa's collection. They're stored right now, but when I get a place of my own again . . ."

Horace smiled sadly. "In storage. I will soon be in storage myself."

Rowen had left the shop and was standing on a corner waiting for the light to change when the thought struck her. He needs a partner! He needs me! He could teach me the business.

She had stood stock still while a tentative enthusiasm seeped into her thoughts. The bookshop would give her a reason for getting up in the mornings. Learning the business would wake up her mind, which her depression seemed to have numbed.

She had turned on her heel, gone back to Horace and made her proposal. He had accepted almost as promptly. Now, months later, she had learned enough to call herself a bibliopole —a dealer in rare books. She wondered if Dave Archer would be impressed, and then laughed at herself. Why would he care?

The blast of an impatient horn brought her to her senses. She shook her head to banish her dangerous imaginings. Friendship led to love. And lovemaking. And betrayal. At least Dave wouldn't object to cats in the bed, she thought, her mind leaping wildly. Her ex-husband had developed, he claimed, an allergy to her two cats. When she learned of his behavior with the starlets he was supposedly filming, she had let the cats into the bedroom and ceased to back his career. In the end, though, she was the one who felt belittled and embittered, the one who lost too much weight.

Certainly she no longer loved Joe. Perhaps she never had, but she had taken the failure of her marriage hard. Thank heaven for the bookshop! With relief she returned her thoughts to the present. Six boxes of books were due to arrive that day. She and Horace would have the joy of unpacking them, perhaps discovering an autograph or a first edition.

The promised delivery arrived late that afternoon as snow was beginning to drift down. The flakes turned to a flurry, then to a full-fledged snowfall, and the weather signaled the end of business for that day.

In the back room of the shop Rowen changed into an old pair of jeans; then she and Horace began to open the crates.

Closing time came. Rowen locked the door against the darkness and falling snow, and she and the old man continued to unpack and talk about the books. Not until her stomach growled did she look at her watch. The hands stood at six o'clock.

"I'm supposed to be someplace!" she exclaimed. Brushing futilely at her jeans, she pondered whether to telephone Dave to say she'd be late or simply get there as fast as possible. She decided her jeans looked all right, considering the nasty weather. Anyhow, it didn't matter how she looked. Vicky was the guest of honor.

Rowen's mind presented her with a vivid picture of Dave as she had seen him the night before, his cheeks reddened by the cold, his wide, handsome mouth smiling. Against her better judgment she was looking forward to seeing him again. Pausing only to extract Horace's promise to leave the other crates until the next day, she hurried Vicky into the night.

The snow, sifting quietly through the aura of streetlights past the bare branches of city trees, was so beautiful that Rowen quickly closed her umbrella and walked with bared head. Snowflakes collected on every horizontal surface, covering for a few hours all the city's grime, touching the old buildings with frosting. Her heart swelled, and she felt surprisingly happy. She hadn't felt like this in years.

By the time she rang Dave's downstairs doorbell she had reopened the umbrella, but too late. Her thick dark hair hung in corkscrews.

Of course Dave lived on the top floor of the old four-story walk-up. When she reached the top of the last flight, he was holding the door open.

"Sorry I'm late," Rowen gasped. "We got a shipment of books, and time just slipped away."

"No sweat. It doesn't hurt stew to cook longer."

Rowen stepped inside, and Dave allowed the bullterrier to sniff his hand before he patted her head.

"Clancy, look here!"

Stretched on his side on the bare floor of the living room, a hound raised his head, observed Vicky for a moment and lay back. His total lack of interest made Rowen smile.

"Not exactly a fireball," Dave remarked, taking her coat. "Hey, you're all wet! Does your umbrella leak?"

"No!" She laughed up at him. "I walked for a while without it, watching the snow fall."

Dave's blue eyes held an arrested expression that she found hard to interpret.

"You look like the little match girl, for Pete's sake!" he commented, his gaze taking her in from head to toe. He moved away to hang up her coat.

"Thanks for the compliment," she snapped.

Dave turned back, his expression noncommittal. "I didn't mean to insult you." He gave her a quizzical look. "You arouse some well-buried protective instinct. Don't worry, I'll keep it under control."

Her annoyance gave way to a wisp of disappointment.

He handed her a jug of red table wine and two glasses. "Here, take this to the studio and pour yourself a glass. I'll bring the food as soon as I toss a salad."

Rowen set the jug and glasses on a sturdy round coffee table laid with mats, eating utensils and a basket of French bread. She caught her scruffy reflection in the uncurtained windows. Her appearance shocked her.

"I'll just comb my hair!" she called, then made for the bathroom at the end of a short hall. She also renewed her makeup and thought she looked considerably improved. Now that she was there, she wanted to look her best, but she had come to that conclusion a little late.

She emerged to find Dave placing bowls of salad on the table. He motioned her to the lounge chair and returned with two steaming plates. The beef and mushrooms swimming in wine sauce made Rowen's mouth water. Dave seated himself on the vintage couch, splashed wine into their glasses and raised his.

"Here's to Vicky. I gave her dog biscuits to make her feel at home."

"I wondered what she was crunching."

The bullterrier's nails clicked as she crossed the floor to sit at Rowen's feet. Dave's hound was apparently too lazy to get up. As Rowen took her first bite of the delicious stew, a striped gray cat emerged from beneath the couch, eyed the visiting dog suspiciously and leapt to the top of a tall file cabinet.

"Well, this is my studio," Dave said. "That's my cat, Harrison."

Rowen looked around the bare room. The corner where they sat included an ugly old floor lamp with a parchment shade. The rest of the furniture consisted of a drawing table, with its own lamp, and the file cabinet. With snow falling silently outside the windows, Rowen almost shivered. No seduction scenes here. Unless, of course, his bedroom was cozier. Was that where he took the women who interested him? Or did he go to their apartments? Envy stabbed her, envy of the carefree women she imagined he knew. He certainly was attractive; his wide mouth and square chin gave him a boy-next-door look. He was wearing well-washed jeans and a thick gray-blue sweater that emphasized the breadth of his chest and his bright blue eyes.

He seemed to expect her to comment on the room.

"It's very . . . businesslike," she managed.

"If I want comfort, I watch television in the bedroom, or read. My desk is there, too." He indicated the couch and chair. "These pieces are really props."

"The bare windows, too?"

Dave nodded, his mouth full of crusty French bread.

"I'd like to see some of your work."

"You will. That's how I intend to entertain you while I sketch Vicky."

"You're really going to draw her, then?"

"Did you think I lured you up here to seduce you?"

"Remember what happened last time you touched me," she warned.

"We could shut the bedroom door." Dave slanted a look at her. Had she expected to be seduced? She was painfully thin—not his type at all. He liked women with interesting curves. And yet . . . There it was again! That feeling of protectiveness. He leapt to his feet, brought the stew pot to the table and ladled more food onto his plate. Her plate was still half full. He'd gone to some trouble to prepare the dinner, and now she didn't seem to care for it.

"Eat up," he ordered. "You need more meat on your bones."

"Drop dead," Rowen said without heat.

"Did I hit a nerve?" He looked at her with such understanding that she caught her breath.

To her surprise, she heard herself explaining. "I went through a very bad divorce a year ago."

"So for the rest of your life you're not going to eat?"

His words made her smile, but she knew her stomach best. "If I swallow any more, I'll be sick. The food was delicious, but . . ."

"All right."

Later he carried their plates and wineglasses to the kitchen. Rowen followed with the other items.

"Coffee?" he asked briskly.

"Please." She glanced at her watch. How long was this going to take? He had made her self-conscious. He wasn't in the least interested in seducing her. It was silly to feel rejected, yet she did. She wanted to get back to the pleasant elegance of her uncle's house and huddle into a big quilted robe that would hide her skinniness, even from herself. She determined to make more of an effort to eat, starting tomorrow.

He settled her on the couch with her coffee, a scrapbook and a printed volume of his work. He explained offhandedly that a second volume was coming out in time for Christmas. Vicky sprawled at Rowen's feet and Dave sketched steadily. From time to time he coaxed Vicky to sit up or change position.

At first Rowen didn't think his cartoons were funny. He drew wacky animals and people in old-fashioned run-down surroundings that were pitiful rather than humorous. But slowly she began to see the poignant humor. One cartoon showed a seedy man coming into a bleak apartment like Dave's, carrying an antique coatrack, telling his dog they were now prepared for company. A spurt of laughter welled within her. His drawings laughed at the tender weirdness of human beings.

From time to time Dave looked up from sketching to watch Rowen's reaction to his jokes. She smiled, and the smile stayed on her face as she turned the pages. Finally she began to laugh. Dave felt an absurd sense of elation. She liked his work!

He began sketching her with Vicky at her feet, trying not for a caricature but for a realistic likeness. She had beautiful features. He would like to see how she looked five pounds heavier. Ten pounds would be about right. She was small boned.

Small breasted, too. The thought leapt to his mind, and he imagined touching her. He would be tender with her, and she would be very sweet, he felt sure of that. He would like to see her brown eyes radiant with fulfillment. He wondered how it would be to wake and find her shining dark hair fanned across his pillow.

The sketch he made of her wasn't satisfactory. He had tried to work too fast, not wanting her to guess he was drawing her as well as her dog. Instead of tearing it up, however, he turned it facedown on his drawing board and concentrated on Vicky.

"How old is she?" he asked.

"A little over a year. She was the cutest puppy!"

"All puppies are cute. Do you know anything about the breed?"

"I do, as it happens. I'll spare you the gruesome details about medieval blood sports, but when dogfighting became popular, bulldogs were too big and slow. So they were crossed with terriers, and bullterriers were the result. They're called pit bulls because they fought in pits. They also put them in with rats, to see how many they could kill in a given time."

"Hey, Vicky, want to go rat hunting some night?"

"I'm sure she'd love it," Rowen said. "Pit bulls are supposed to be gallant and ready for combat."

"How well I know!"

Rowen raised her head with a smile that made his heart beat faster. Whatever it was that attracted him, he was in a fair way to feeling more interest than he wished. To counter such thoughts he began asking questions.

"What did you think of them?"

"They're good. All of them. I can see why you're successful."

"I make enough to support myself, though this isn't exactly grandeur."

"Ever been married?" she inquired.

Dave shook his head and gave a wry smile. "I can't afford to marry. The woman who gets me will have to be rich."

Rowen's heart jolted. Had he guessed the truth about her? Common sense quickly asserted itself. He hadn't guessed anything.

"In other words, you're not serious about women," she said succinctly.

"That's the truth," Dave muttered. Being responsible for Karen had taught him a lot.

"Most women support themselves nowadays."

"They do when you meet them," Dave conceded. "Then they start getting tired of their jobs, or they want to have a baby, or they want you to move to Santa Fe." Listening to himself, Dave felt sure he meant every word.

Rowen's heart sank for no accountable reason. Beyond paying back a debt, she had no interest in this man. Nevertheless, she wanted to upset his smug self-satisfaction. "Don't you get lonely?" she needled.

"For female companionship? No. It's as close as the nearest singles bar. Or I meet other commercial artists at a bar on Third Avenue where they go to get away from their live-in girl friends."

"You sound very cynical."

"I am," he said, then realized he was putting on an act for her benefit, and laughed at himself. "What's all this cross-examination?" he joked. "You're not in the market. You're still mourning the last fellow."

"What makes you think that?"

"Losing weight, not eating."

"That's not the reason!"

"What, then? Are you short of money?" Dave looked up from his sketch, his eyes boring into hers.

She was too taken aback to answer.

Dave said, "Clerking in a used-book store can't be the most profitable job in the world."

"It's not a used-book store! We specialize in rare volumes."

"Too bad you can't eat books. It's obvious you don't take care of yourself."

Rowen's highly paid family physician had told her the same thing, but coming from Dave, she found the advice infuriating.

"That's not your business!" she snapped. "I do all right."

Dave laughed at her spurt of temper. "You're full of spunk, anyhow. How about another glass of wine?"

"I'll get it," she offered. Let him finish drawing so she could get out of there.

"Do you mind?" He flashed her a grin. "It's in the refrigerator."

"You shouldn't keep red wine in the refrigerator. It's supposed to be at room temperature."

"What do I know about keeping wine? I'm a country boy from Missouri. Ask me about moonshine."

She smiled and stepped into the kitchen. She heard him crossing the floor behind her.

"Don't you think I can find the refrigerator?" she demanded.

"I needed a stretch." He lounged in the doorway. He liked seeing a woman in his kitchen. Not to do the work, but because it was cozier. He'd be the first to agree that men and women were meant to live together. If only togetherness didn't get so complicated!

Rowen opened the refrigerator and looked for the wine bottle. In front of the ordinary contents a woman's hand dangled, hanging by a string attached to the cutoff wrist.

"Eeee!"

She slammed the door, punctuating her shriek. Then her

30

mind readjusted the glimpse she had taken. The hand was plaster—a hand for a mannequin. Hysterical laughter burst from her even while she shuddered.

"I'm sorry!" Dave exclaimed, but he was unable to suppress a grin. He moved around her to take out the jug. "I forgot that was in there."

"Ooooh! How could you!" She shuddered and hugged herself. "Did you do that on purpose to hear me scream?"

"No! I forgot about it. Honestly."

"What's it for, then? To scare icebox raiders?"

"No." Dave laughed. He poured two glasses of wine and handed her one. "Here—I guess you need this. I hang it in various places. It reminds me that things out of their expected place are the essence of humor."

"I feel sorry for your cleaning lady."

"What makes you think I have a cleaning lady? Don't you think I'm capable?" In the confined space of the kitchen he slipped a casual arm about her.

The kitchen floor seemed to spin, and Dave's arm was like a safe haven. She wanted to lean against him. Instead she twisted away.

"I'm sure you are. I just assumed you had someone." Rowen absently took a piece of the crusty bread to go with her wine and strolled back to the couch. Dave returned to his drawing table.

As she watched Dave draw, she thought that she had never met anyone so interesting. Too bad their acquaintance was to be so brief. He didn't seem inclined to talk while he worked, so Rowen wandered to the window and looked out at the snow. "It's melting as fast as it falls," she reported.

"Want to watch television?" Dave asked absentmindedly. "Go in the bedroom. The bed's made—and not by the cleaning lady."

"Sorry. I didn't mean to imply you were helpless."

She did want to see his bedroom. Her coat lay on the bed, atop a puffy comforter with earth-colored stripes. She looked around the room. She was glad to see he didn't live as starkly as his studio indicated. Unsurprised, she noted Dave's cat curled on her coat. Bolsters matching the comforter made the bed a cozy lounge. A television set stood on a dresser for easy viewing. Curtains hung at the window, a cheerful red rug covered most of the floor. The room looked neat and masculine.

She turned on the TV—her reason for being there—and continued to look around. His clothes were put away. She noted with approval that his desk looked neat, but not too neat. For some inexplicable reason she felt glad to know he looked after himself well. He was a competent person. Responsible.

As soon as she settled on the bed she heard the click of Vicky's nails on the bare floor outside. A white muzzle appeared at the edge of the bed.

"It's no good without you." Dave lounged in the doorway. "She won't stay put," he explained.

"Ohhh!" Rowen swung her feet off the bed and took the white muzzle in both hands. "Vicky, don't you realize you're a model?"

The white tail wagged; the little eyes gazed into Rowen's with devotion. She glanced at her watch. "We really should be getting home."

"I suppose so." Dave wondered why he felt reluctant to see her go. "I really appreciate this. I hope you weren't too bored."

"No. I hope you got some good sketches."

"I did. I see the cat found your coat. Sorry."

"Don't worry. I'm used to cats."

"I'll walk you home." Dave took his coat from the closet.

"That's not necessary," she said, but something inside her leapt at the prospect.

"I know, but Clancy hasn't been out. Besides, I want to."

The snow had stopped. Ordinarily Rowen would have found the cold damp air and wet sidewalks grim. Tonight, walking beside Dave, she found the air exhilarating. She felt almost happy. Dave's lighthearted mood affected her, too. She laughed at his sallies and said a couple of things that made him chuckle.

"Sutton Place!" He sounded annoyed as they turned the corner. "And I thought you didn't have enough to eat!"

"I'm house-sitting," she explained quickly. "And I *do* have enough to eat!"

She stopped before her door and gave him her hand.

"What is this—good-bye?" Dave asked. "I was hoping you'd bring Vicky back if I promise to make you dinner again."

"I could . . ." She stopped, though she wanted very much to accept.

"How about Wednesday?"

"Wednesday's okay," she admitted, as was any other night, if he but knew.

"Great! I'll see you both then." Warm lips touched her cold cheek as she fumbled for her key.

"Good night," she said tautly when the door swung open.

He waved. "See you Wednesday!"

Inside she closed the door and leaned against it, happy but scared. Was she going to be foolish enough to get involved with a man again? But this one should be safe enough. She smiled wryly. He wasn't even interested in her, only in Vicky.

3

I'm not interested in her!" Dave said to himself as he and Clancy strolled home. "Why did I commit myself? I don't need more sketches of Vicky. Tomorrow evening I'll call and cancel. No, damnit, I can't!" He had forgotten to get her telephone number. That showed how uninterested he really was.

An hour later, while brushing his teeth, he caught himself busily planning what to cook for her. It occurred to him that he should invite someone else, as well. The atmosphere wouldn't be so intimate. He dithered, reluctant for some reason to introduce her to any of his male friends.

In an act of swift decision he picked up the telephone and called Mel, a draftsman he sometimes went drinking with. Mel was divorced, had a steady job and could be considered fairly reliable. It wouldn't be right to introduce Rowen to some deadbeat. God, was he already feeling responsible for her?

Mel picked up the phone, relieving him of the necessity of answering that question.

"Mel, old buddy. How about coming to dinner Wednesday night . . . ? The occasion? Nothing much. I've got a woman coming. I invited her up because she owns this absurd dog I wanted to draw. Skinny little thing. Not the dog, the woman." He was patient while Mel made a ribald comment. "Well, you know how it is, she wangled another invitation. Actually, I thought you might like to meet her. You go for the wan, helpless type. No, I'm not having steaks! I'm making Missouri church supper casserole—hamburger, cheese, tomatoes and green peppers, baked with spaghetti. . . . Sure, goes great with beer. . . . Bring beer or wine. . . . How do I know? They don't drink either one at church suppers!"

He hung up. Instead of feeling pleased, he felt ashamed—of himself, of the impression he had given Mel. Rowen hadn't wangled an invitation; she hadn't even hinted that she wanted to see him again. That's what was bugging him! Why hadn't she wanted to see him again? He was pretending she *had* hinted so that ending their acquaintance could be his choice.

Why didn't she like him?

"What's not to like?" he demanded of Clancy.

He shook his head at his own folly and resolved to stop thinking about her.

Actually, Rowen was looking forward to seeing Dave again, all too aware that it was a dangerous pleasure. But surely one more evening wouldn't get her into trouble. Afterward he would be through with Vicky and that would be the end.

On the appointed evening she arrived fifteen minutes early. She allowed herself the extra time because this would be her last visit. It wouldn't hurt to indulge.

Vicky went up the four flights of stairs at top speed, as though she remembered the dog biscuits. The result was that Rowen arrived at Dave's door breathless. When he opened it, the sight of him took what little breath she had left. He seemed bigger, better looking, more vital. Maybe she was contrasting him with Horace. At seventy-eight, people didn't look vital.

"Making up for last week?" Dave inquired.

"What do you mean?"

"You're early." He felt absurdly pleased at the prospect of

having her to himself for a quarter of an hour. Unless Mel arrived ahead of time, too. He found himself thinking of Mel as being in the way, a bit of a nuisance. What had made him include a third person?

Rowen thrust a bag holding a bottle into his hands and unsnapped Vicky's leash.

"I didn't know whether to bring red wine or white," she explained. "You don't have to open it tonight if it doesn't go with the meal."

She looked so serious that Dave smothered a smile. "Red or white—it'll get drunk! It's easy to see you haven't been around artists."

She went to put her coat in the bedroom. In the kitchen he laughed to himself and took out the bottle. Red wine—good! Cabernet sauvignon, but not one he was familiar with. A sales slip fell out of the bag. With reprehensible curiosity Dave glanced at it. Fifteen dollars! No wonder he wasn't familiar with it.

She's extravagant, he thought with disapproval. House-sitting on Sutton Place indicated she had dreams of grandeur.

He patted Vicky and gave her a dog biscuit. The casserole was in the oven; the salad was ready to be tossed. He opened the bottle and filled two glasses, then carried them into the studio, feeling as though he were putting one over on Mel. He shook his head at himself, but still he sat down to enjoy the time alone with Rowen.

She saw the extra place setting and cocked her head like a bright-eyed sparrow. "Someone else must be coming."

"A friend I owe dinner to. He does layouts for a big ad agency. Nice guy. I thought as long as I was cooking . . ." His voice trailed away. Sometimes his ideas were very stupid. He raised his glass.

"Here's to many sketches of Vicky."

Rowen relaxed. At least he hadn't invited a second woman—a girl friend—as she had feared when she saw the third plate.

Sitting across the low table from her, Dave studied her appearance the way he did everything that came under his eye.

Crazy thoughts chased through his mind—the idea of kissing her, of gathering her up and setting her on his lap. Hah! That would go over well with a liberated female! She would probably throw the wine in his face.

Oh, well. His ruminations took a humorous twist. Despite Saint Paul's pronouncement, what a man thought in his heart wasn't the same as following up on it. If that were true, the world *would* be a mess. He wrenched his mind away from such thoughts and made a remark about the day's springlike weather.

"Did you think of any cartoons to use Vicky in?" Rowen inquired.

"Not yet. I trust she's been behaving herself with strangers," he said heartily. "I'd hate to think she takes up with every man she sees."

"Oh, no. She's very discriminating." Rowen's smile lit her thin face and brought a glow to her eyes. Her teeth were white and even. Dave could almost see her as a skinny little girl with braces.

"Did you find any rare editions this week?"

"No." She smiled again.

He realized he wanted to hear how she'd been spending her time and decided to ask directly. "What have you been doing since I last saw you?"

Her eyes were wandering around the studio. She brought them back to his face in surprise. "Doing?"

"Yes. Your weekend," he prompted.

"Oh . . ." She frowned, not wanting to admit that she had spent most of Sunday at the shop, rearranging books. Celia had gone skiing in Vermont. Should she say she had gone, too? But she didn't want to lie to him; she wasn't going to pretend she was the outgoing type. "I did some work at the shop," she said vaguely. "Then I took Vicky for a walk in the park. What have you been doing?"

Dave shrugged. "Hanging around. Thinking." He wondered whether to try to tell her what dull agony it was, trying to come up with cartoon ideas. You could read over your whole joke collection, hoping for a new angle; you could read the news; you could look through notes you'd made, but in the end you sat at the drawing table, doodling, hoping that the oft-drawn light bulb would appear over your head. Going out and getting drunk or taking a woman to bed only put off the evil hour. Eventually you had to sit down and *think*. At least, that was the way it worked for him. Very few of his ideas came easily.

He opened his mouth to explain this, but the buzzer sounded.

"That'll be Mel." He buzzed to open the door, then returned to the studio to enjoy a last moment alone with Rowen. He savored the smooth dry taste of the wine and thought it went with Rowen's personality. Quiet, unassuming, exclusive.

Mel came in on a draft of cold air, his dark eyes bright, his nose red from the falling temperature. He handed Dave a six-pack of beer, but on seeing the wineglasses he decided to drink wine, too.

Dave took his guest's coat and introduced him to Rowen and Vicky.

Mel was a studious-looking man of about Rowen's age, with a thin black mustache and thick rimless glasses. He struck her as very neat; no doubt he made neat, careful drawings. He wore a dark tie and a striped shirt, having come straight from work. He had a ready laugh, and as soon as he joined Rowen on the lumpy couch Vicky came over to him to be petted.

"Look at that!" Dave exclaimed. "I hope you're flattered! She *bit* me."

"Where was this?" Mel inquired.

Rowen spoke up in defense of her dog. "On Third Avenue. He was a complete stranger, and he came up and grabbed me."

"Rowen slipped on some ice. I saved her from falling," Dave protested.

"A likely story!" Mel teased his friend. "To look at him, you wouldn't think he'd have to resort to scare tactics, but you never know. Some have it, some haven't."

Dave grinned good-naturedly. "My approach works. Vicky and Rowen are both here."

Mel took an appreciative swallow of wine and glanced at his watch. "Listen, if we get through eating in time, I've got three tickets to an Off-Off-Broadway production. The boss brought them around right before quitting time. We did some work for the producer. I don't guarantee anything. It's a preview."

"Where?"

"Downtown. Somewhere in the East Village."

"I'll dish up, then." Dave went off to the kitchen. Rowen followed, offering to help. He sent her back with the salad, and they sat down to the meal.

"Say, this is good!" Mel exclaimed after his first forkful.

"It is good," Rowen seconded, but looking at her plate, she felt her self-confidence drain away. Dave had given her a huge serving. She got the message without being hit over the head: He considered her too skinny. He probably liked strapping, voluptuous women. All artists did, judging by the models they painted. He himself was so big and good-natured and easy-going. He would go for the earthy type.

Mel and Dave ate fast, not doing justice to the well-cooked meal. Rowen followed their lead. There was no dessert, though Dave offered coffee.

"There's cheese and fruit," he explained, "but if you have it now, you'll be late for the play. How about when you come back?"

"We!" Mel exclaimed. "Aren't you going?"

"I think you two should go. I'll stay and draw Vicky."

Rowen felt sharp disappointment, followed by anger. How dare he invite her to dinner and foist her off on someone else! To hide her reaction she turned to Mel with an outward show of enthusiasm. "I've never seen anything Off-Off-Broadway. Maybe it'll turn out to be a hit!"

"Yeah," Mel seconded. "Dave will be sorry then."

"I would be," Dave agreed with a grin. He carried the last dishes to the kitchen as Mel went to fetch Rowen's and his coats.

Dave returned from the kitchen and bent his friendly blue gaze on Rowen. She felt swept by something out of her control.

"You don't mind, do you?" he asked. "It'll be more fun than sitting around watching me draw. Mel's a good guy."

"I'm sure it will be fun," she said, her eyes bright with anger. "But I would have preferred to have a choice in the matter." From the corner of her eye she saw Mel coming with their coats. "Vicky, be good!" she admonished the dog. Then she slid her arms into the coat Mel was holding, and he swept her out the door.

In the taxi going downtown Mel was amusing and entertaining. Rowen was relieved when he didn't try to hold her hand, didn't treat her like a date. He probably felt awkward, too. They were being shunted off to the theater like two kids in the grown-ups' way.

She gave a disgruntled sigh.

Mel sensed the cause of her annoyance. "Pretty high-handed of Dave, sending us off. I wasn't dead set on seeing the play. I had the tickets, so I mentioned it. I hope you don't mind."

Rowen did mind, but she was too well bred to say so. It wasn't Mel's fault. Either Dave should have come, too, or they all should have stayed at the studio. She and Mel could have entertained each other. She was going to have a word or two to say to Dave. If she got the chance.

What made her think she'd have a chance? He'd made it pretty clear that he wasn't interested. She wished he hadn't bothered to hunt her down after their first meeting, or gone to the trouble of cooking.

The play turned out to be terrible.

"I feel sorry for anybody who paid for these tickets," Mel muttered during the first intermission. "Do you want to leave?"

Rowen saw other people gathering their wraps and shook her head. "I couldn't do that to the actors. It's not their fault the play's lousy."

They left their coats on their seats and strolled into the lobby, where Mel bought plastic glasses of red wine. Rowen sipped hers and made a face. Mel laughed.

She apologized quickly. "It wasn't what I expected."

"Did you expect it to be as good as the wine you brought to dinner?"

"Maybe." She smiled. "Have you known Dave long?" Her pulse fluttered ridiculously as she said his name.

"About five years. He used to do temporary work in my department. He could have had a full-time job there, but he'd rather free-lance his cartoons. He's done well—I've got to give him credit. He has his own weird sense of humor, that's for sure."

Rowen thought of Dave's cartoons—the seedy characters with their demented dogs and rooms full of cats. She agreed wholeheartedly.

"He's a great friend, though. A guy you can count on. When my wife left me, Dave called every night. He'd listen to me talk, or we'd eat out or get drunk. Sometimes we just sat and watched TV." Mel smiled reminiscently. "He was the only one of my so-called friends who gave a damn. The rest of them acted embarrassed. Like I let them down by being cut up when my marriage ended."

"I was cut up when mine ended, too," Rowen murmured sympathetically.

"See! Women can admit it. Men are supposed to hang tough and get ulcers."

"I hope you avoided the ulcers!"

"Yeah. I came to see the whole thing was for the best. I mean, she's got what she wants now—a house in the suburbs, close to her mother's—and I've got a chance to look around. Same with Dave."

"Was he married?"

"No, but he had a longtime, live-in girl friend. I always thought she was a pain in the neck, but he felt responsible. . . ."

The lights dimmed. Mel broke off his interesting confidence, and they returned to their seats. Rowen nodded to herself. Aunt Helen was right when she said men gossiped as much as women.

Throughout the second act she thought about Dave. What it

would be like to live with him, to wake up in that cozy bedroom and spend her evenings—where? In the bare studio? In bed, reading? There wasn't much choice. If Mel's apartment was furnished like Dave's, she could understand why his wife had left for the suburbs.

I'd insist on a bigger place, Rowen concluded idly. She knew couples who had acquired condos or apartments side by side and combined them.

Dave had not behaved well tonight. She brooded on his behavior. She wished Mel had finished his confidence about Dave's girl friend. She wondered what the woman looked like. Like herself, maybe? Could she be his type at all?

As the curtain fell on the second of three acts, Mel muttered, "Polite or not, let's go! It'll be late enough by the time we finish sitting around at Dave's drinking coffee. I assume you have to work tomorrow, too. I can't see losing sleep for this bomb."

Rowen was easily convinced. She couldn't help wondering how Dave and Vicky were getting along.

Dave's evening had been uneasy. At first Vicky had stalked back and forth like a prisoner. She had looked at Dave as though to ask why her mistress had abandoned her in a strange place. Finally she had grown tired of stalking and lain down just long enough for Dave to start a sketch. Then, at the sound of someone on the stairs, she had leapt to her feet. It had happened again and again. At last Dave had thrown down his pencil and gotten out his Polaroid camera.

By degrees he had become aware that he, too, was awaiting Rowen's return. Something about her—her big brown eyes or her little match girl look—went straight to his heart.

He had thought of Mel and could have ground his teeth. Old Mel would be making the best of his opportunity—it wasn't every day he got introduced to a woman like Rowen, one without any crazy quirks. Mel would know how to respond. He'd probably hold her hand all through the play, kiss her in the taxi, make a date for next week. *He* wouldn't forget to ask for

her phone number. *He* wouldn't have hang-ups about responsibility. He had a good job.

Dave had reviewed again his arguments against working
full-time. In the first place, he couldn't do layouts all day and
come home and be creative at night. And weekends weren't
long enough. You barely got started and it was Sunday night.
And when were you supposed to indulge in a little recreation
and make the human contacts necessary for coming up with
gags?

Vicky interrupted his mental review by pacing. She prowled
to the door and whined.

"Not yet," Dave told her. She continued to whine, and his
own ears pricked.

A knock sounded on his door, and Mel called, "We're back!
Open up!"

Vicky pranced in circles of excitement and uttered little yelps.
Dave opened the door and saw Rowen behind Mel. His heart
behaved as ridiculously as Vicky. It leapt and thudded as
though their separation had dragged as endlessly for him as for
the dog.

"Come in." He looked at her, pink-cheeked and bright-eyed,
and longed to plant a kiss—kisses—on her breathless mouth. If
his expression was giving him away, he didn't care.

"Play any good?" he asked, suppressing a tremor in his
voice.

"Lousy," Mel said. "You shouldn't have sent us off."

"Sent *you* off! Who had the tickets? I suppose you'd have
liked me to suffer, too." He aimed a playful punch at Mel's
shoulder, a wonderful release for his taut nerves. "Okay, more
wine, crackers and cheese? Or would you prefer coffee?"

Rowen squatted down to fuss over Vicky.

"She really missed you," Dave babbled. "We both did," he
added when Mel's back was turned.

Rowen's surprised dark eyes scanned him. Their glances
caught and held while she stood up slowly. Vicky pranced
about her, wagging and snuffling, but the dog and everything

else dropped into the background. Rowen's eyes locked with his and nothing else existed. She seemed to know what he had been through in the last two hours. He couldn't believe it, yet the knowledge was there, as sure as they stood toe to toe.

Mel returned from the bathroom. Dave was still staring at Rowen as though entranced.

"Rowen, aren't you going to take your coat off?" Mel asked. "Hey, Dave, where's that coffee you promised?"

Dave moved then. "Rowen—" He put out a hand to touch her, to keep her from walking away. She looked back at him over her shoulder, but she was already laughing at something Mel had said.

Shaken and bemused, Dave filled the teakettle and turned on the burner, hardly knowing what he was doing. He had heard of people being love struck—was this it? Dismay overrode his surging excitement. But the attraction was there—strong and sweet and exciting. He felt glad, and at the same time confused.

Love . . . Rowen thought. A vast tidal wave seemed to have swept her into its power, overwhelming her and Dave both. His gaze had met and fused with hers like drops of mercury uniting. Was it only a split-second, freakish occurrence? She certainly hoped so, because it was frightening to imagine where such a tidal wave might take her. In a brief flash of imagination she saw her body tossed broken and lifeless against a pile of debris—a picture culled from some television news report of a disaster. And disaster it would be if she let herself be swept away by someone so remote from her world. His strange life-style was what attracted her, she told herself. Only that. Of course, he *was* very good looking. And he had a certain charm.

With a mental shake she made herself stop appraising his good points. The fact was that he awoke sensations that were safer buried.

Dave didn't talk much over the crackers and cheese, but gradually Rowen's tension eased. She countered Mel's stories about foul-ups at work with some about the shop.

Nevertheless, it was a relief when she was able at last to put on her coat and snap Vicky's leash. She wanted to be alone, to hug her secret and dwell on it. Dave *must* feel the same way she did—right? She wanted to explore the sensation of being bowled over. She needed to know if her rational mind had actually been left helpless in the face of sudden passion. She hoped that the dangerous sensation would waft away like a wisp of fog along the early-morning Connecticut shore.

Outside the wind was bitter, and it had begun to snow. They all called good-night as Mel set off into the face of the wind. Dave offered to walk Rowen home, but he had come out without a cap or muffler, and Clancy was shivering. Neither of them spoke of what had happened upstairs.

A taxi came, chains jangling on the packed snow. Rowen hailed it.

Dave seemed to emerge from a daze. "Hey!" He raised his voice above the howling wind. "I still don't have your phone number." He hauled a pad and pencil from his pocket and scribbled it down.

While the taxi waited, he pulled Rowen into his arms. His kiss was hard and quick.

"I'll call you!" he promised.

In the cab Rowen gave the driver her address and sank back, thinking about the curious thing that had happened.

She went to sleep that night warmed by a strange glow.

Next morning, on her walk to work, experience and reality began to assert their power. Being overcome by another person was crazy and dangerous. It could lead to unhappiness and misery. Better to go to bed lonely than to lie, anguished, waiting for someone who didn't come.

She told Vicky that the look that had passed between her and Dave was nothing . . . something she had imagined. But accepting that explanation meant denying the strongest intuition she had ever experienced.

That evening she read the review of a new comedy playing on Broadway. She told Celia she'd like to see it. Celia, always up on everything, had already been.

"Get your cartoonist to take you," Celia suggested. "It's right up his alley. Humor," she explained.

"Call up and ask him to take me? I couldn't do it."

"So take him," Celia said, bored.

Something leapt inside Rowen, but something else resisted.

"Tell him a friend couldn't use the tickets," Celia said patiently.

"I know that's what the magazine articles suggest, but I don't think I could. I'd die if he refused."

"He won't refuse. He'll be flattered. You know something? Men don't know how to say no. Women . . . we learn from the time we're in grade school how to turn boys down nicely, but guys never get that practice. Go on—order two tickets and call him."

"I don't want him to take me out because he can't say no!" Rowen protested and walked out of the room.

Upstairs in her bedroom she undressed, quickly covering her slight body with a frothy nightgown and peignoir. She sat in the frilly slipper chair, looking as fragile as a Dresden shepherdess —a brooding shepherdess. Dave hadn't really liked her. All he'd thought about was drawing Vicky.

She studied her arm judiciously. If only she weren't so thin! A few years ago she'd had a nice figure, but now . . . Face it, she told herself. The most attractive thing about you is your money. Without that no man will look at you twice.

Dave did, another voice said.

Something stronger than self-disparagement made her want to do something for him. He should keep abreast of current trends in humor. She felt pretty sure he couldn't afford the price of a Broadway play. It would be a way to repay his hospitality. He had cooked for her twice, and he had made her feel like a woman again.

No! She set her jaw. She didn't want to feel like a woman. That was too painful. What she wanted to do was pay attention to her bookshop and succeed at it. She'd had enough of being used. Men used women.

Not all men, a whisper of reality interrupted. Some men. . . .

No more dreams! She rushed into the bathroom and began brushing her teeth. Toothbrushing, that was reality.

He telephoned her at work. She was in the middle of waiting on a customer and had to ask Dave to wait. While she finished the sale her breath seemed to stop. What was he going to say? What was *she* going to say?

His speech almost stilted, he asked her if she would care to have dinner with him on Saturday night. The fearful expectancy she felt as she said yes was like the downhill rush on a roller coaster.

"Thank you," she added formally. The silence on the other end seemed to stretch for an eternity. Rowen gulped and tried to fill it.

"Oh, Saturday! Listen, I might have two tickets for that new Broadway comedy for Saturday. Some friends bought tickets, but now they may be going out of town. Would you—" She had to draw a breath. "Would you want to go?"

"You bet!" His alarming stiffness melted. "I've been dying to see it. What a piece of luck! That you got the tickets, I mean. I'm lucky, too, that you're willing to go out with me after the other night. . . ."

"What do you mean?"

"Sending you off with Mel to that lousy show. I thought you might decide to cross me off."

"Not quite." Rowen laughed breathlessly.

Dave seemed to remember suddenly that she was at work. "I'd better get off the phone and let you tend to business." They decided on the time he would pick her up, and the conversation ended.

For a few moments Rowen sat in a daze of delight. Then she started out of her daze and began phoning ticket agents.

She spent the intervening days deciding what to wear. She wanted something elegant and dressy, but bare shoulders would emphasize her thinness, and the theatre would be cold. She spent lunch searching the Madison Avenue boutiques. She found a sheer dark dress with spaghetti straps and a matching long-sleeved jacket. The jacket fastened at the waist, leaving her throat and the upper curves of her breasts bare. Her sparkling diamond pendant and matching earrings looked marvelous with it, but she laid them aside in favor of pearls. Even a shop girl could afford fake pearls, and Dave wouldn't notice whether they were real or not, or that the dress was expensive.

He arrived at the Sutton Place house dressed for a night out and looking handsome. The sheepskin coat had been replaced by a trench coat over a blue turtleneck sweater and a tweed sports jacket. For once Dave's hair didn't look as if he'd been running his fingers through it. He had changed his boots for nicely polished loafers. In fact, he had gone to the trouble of getting dressed up.

He took her to a small French restaurant near the theater. The food was good, but the tables were crowded so closely together that it was a major effort to slide between them. Intimacy was impossible; it was all one could do not to join the conversation at the next table.

"What have you been doing since I last saw you?" Dave asked. If they had been alone, she might have looked him in the eyes and said, "Thinking of you." Instead she said, "Nothing much. I went to a party at the Frick Museum."

"I read about that!" Dave's eyebrows shot up. "A special showing of medieval manuscripts for the patrons. Before they let in the unwashed. You're not a patron?"

"Uh . . . no! I . . ." Rowen realized she had fumbled and searched her brain for an explanation. "The people where I'm staying . . . The invitation arrived . . . I'm supposed to open any mail that isn't personal, and I thought, why not?"

Dave grinned. "Party crasher! I knew there was something wicked about you the first time I saw you. I hope you ate lots of hors d'oeuvres and drank all their champagne."

Never in her life had Rowen thought of crashing a party. More often than not she tried to avoid the society functions to which she was invited. Sudden worry lines gave a pinched look to her lovely face.

Dave wondered what he'd said wrong. She must get a kick out of hobnobbing with the wealthy. If so, she would drop him fast enough. Or had she gone for the food? He didn't care what she claimed, she wasn't eating enough!

Rowen searched wildly for a change of subject. "We found a genuine autographed Whitman this week. That is, Horace did, my partner."

"Found it?"

"In a box of old books. 'Found' meaning the people who sold the box probably didn't know the Whitman was there."

"That must have been exciting!" Dave's face radiated interest. That, Rowen reflected, was what made him so attractive. He entered into the spirit of things. She felt bad about lying to him about the patrons' party, but she had set out to succeed or fail on her own charms.

"It *was* exciting." A swift smile banished her frown of discomfort. "I don't think there's anything like it. It's like finding buried treasure. I'm sure that's what's kept my partner young."

Dave took a thoughtful bite of roast beef. "Your partner?"

Rowen swallowed her forkful of *coq au vin* with difficulty. "I call him my partner," she said lamely. "He's teaching me the business."

Dave gave her a fatherly glance. "Look, you don't have to impress me."

She felt her cheeks burn. Putting quite the opposite meaning on her slip-up, he thought she was trying to make her job sound important. Two slip-ups in half an hour. If she intended to keep this charade intact all evening, she'd have to be more careful. She was relieved when Dave asked a question she could answer honestly—where her name came from.

"My father wanted me named Rowena for his mother. My mother couldn't stand it, so they compromised on Rowen. Rowena is from *Ivanhoe,* remember?"

Dave shook his head. "I wasn't much of a reader. I always had a pencil in my hand, or a felt marker. I like the name Rowen. It's different; it suits you."

Finally they finished eating and set out for the theater. The chance for asking personal questions was over.

It was delightful to sit with Dave waiting for the houselights to dim. She had carefully chosen medium-priced seats. She didn't want him to get the impression that the friends who had "given" her the tickets were well-to-do.

They were early; to fill the time Dave pulled a pad from his pocket and began to draw. He showed her the caricatures as he did them and made her guess which person the sketch represented.

The curtain rose and the play began. It was a joy to be with someone who enjoyed it so much. It was impossible not to join in Dave's ringing laughter. Rowen watched him as much as she watched the stage. He was so handsome and vital, so carefree. She had never laughed so wholeheartedly. It *was* a funny play, but sharing it with Dave made it seem even better. She thought the women around her looked envious.

"Oh!" he gasped at the first intermission, his face alight. "This is great! Be sure to thank your friends. They don't know what they're missing."

At the end they left the theater still laughing. The night was crisp and clear. Talking animatedly, Dave pulled Rowen's arm through his. They walked to Forty-second Street and turned eastward. Happiness welled in Rowen's chest, and the city seemed part of her joy. The lights made her think of diamonds scattered on velvet. She sighed with contentment and said, "Sometimes Manhattan seems to glitter with magic."

"Is it that way for you, too?" Dave asked, his voice tinged with surprise.

"Sometimes."

"I didn't mean constantly," Dave agreed with a laugh. "Not in July, for instance, in the subway."

His remark shattered Rowen's bemused happiness. She could count on one hand the number of times she had been in a subway. Certainly never in July.

Casually she asked Dave what his last cartoons had been

about. He began telling her in detail. Some sounded genuinely funny. At others she laughed politely. Some she didn't understand at all, but she adored listening to him. Dave wasn't put out when she didn't find them all funny. Before they knew it, they were at the corner of Third Avenue.

They went on to First and caught an uptown bus.

As they climbed aboard Rowen thought, *At least by listening to Dave I'm not putting my foot in my mouth or telling more lies.*

Happy as she was, an uncomfortable lump lay inside her. This deception couldn't go on. In a careless moment she had decided she was going to be known only for herself, but it wasn't as easy as that. It meant telling lies, and she didn't like lying. Of course, men lied to women. For example, her ex-husband.

She couldn't tell Dave the truth! It would be better simply not to see him again. The kindest thing would be to end the relationship before it started. She should . . . But she feared that she wasn't tough enough.

They left the bus and walked to her street. At the tiny park at the end of the street they looked at the wide, dark river below. The wind was sharper there. Rowen shivered.

"Are you cold?" Dave turned her to face him. "Why didn't you say something? We could have taken a taxi. Instead you let me talk your ear off. Here. . . ." He tugged her knitted mohair cap down over her ears. Against her chin she felt the cold touch of his suede glove as he pulled her coat collar closer about her throat.

"I feel like I'm being sent out to play." She was smiling when she heard his sharply indrawn breath.

His hand tightened on her collar as he pulled her toward him. His mouth came down on hers—his lips cold, yet fiery. She opened her arms, and he caught her hard against him, his kiss fierce. She couldn't associate this suddenly serious, passionate man with her laughing companion of a moment before. The intensity of his kiss told her that she hadn't been alone in that moment of revelation three nights ago. Emotion had swept Dave, too. An all-encompassing wonder made her hug him tighter.

The layers of down and trench coat, tweed wool and cable knit that separated their bodies mattered not a whit. Dave, too, seemed to know that something tremendous had struck them.

Their tongues met, and loved, and promised. The kiss went on and on. Dave seemed to be saying they had all the time in the world, nothing needed to be rushed. They would explore this wonderful thing that had happened to them tomorrow and in all the days that followed.

At last he raised his head and folded Rowen against him. She felt him laugh shakily.

"I don't know . . ." he said in wonder. "Every time I see you it's so earth-shattering it scares me. Do you feel it, too?"

She nodded mutely. The ache that had troubled her all the way home had eased. Things might work out. This strong, unexpected tie between them demanded to be explored.

"Knowing you takes getting used to," Dave muttered. "I never felt this way about a woman."

"I never felt this way, either," she agreed in a solemn voice.

"But it's wonderful! I never felt so great!" Dave suddenly swung her into his arms. Laughing, he ran with her down the middle of the empty street. "Whatever it is, it's wonderful!"

She shrieked, then remembered the lateness of the hour and gasped. Her cry echoed from the darkened houses. Dave's footsteps rang on the frozen pavement.

"Put me down!" she whispered. "Dave! Everybody can hear us!"

Dave looked suddenly sheepish. Giggling, they tiptoed to Rowen's front door. He waited until she had turned the key in the lock before taking her in his arms again.

His lips were cool fire, like a magician's spell. They set up a tingling that went through her from head to toe. Clothing and time were barriers that only postponed the magic of their knowledge of each other. The outcome was inevitable. Spiritually, they were already entwined. No way in the world could she shake his hand and say a final good-bye.

His good-night kiss left her limp. Were Dave's knees trembling too? He seemed to take a moment to gather himself. He drew a tremulous breath and clipped her under the chin with one gloved finger.

"Thanks for the play, beautiful." He walked away, then looked back over his shoulder. He saw her watching and threw her a kiss. There was no question in Rowen's mind. Whatever was going to happen between them would happen. She was powerless to stop it.

4

Dave woke suddenly in the middle of the night. The quilt had slipped to the floor. He tugged it back onto the bed, dislodging Clancy. The hound had moved to the floor with the quilt, possibly to escape Dave's restlessness.

Sleepily he tried to think why he should have woken up. And then remembered.

Rowen!

His exhilaration of a few hours before came back with a rush. He drew a sharp breath, recalling the excited, half-crazy way he had felt when he took her in his arms. She had seemed to belong to him, as though he had found a part of himself that he hadn't known was missing.

I must have been out of my mind, he thought muzzily. Warmed by the puffy quilt and the memory of Rowen's scent and lips, he slept again.

In the clear cold light of Sunday morning he had second thoughts. In fact, he was scared. What had happened last night? He didn't want to think about it. He had behaved as though he'd drunk too much. Had he really considered proposing? Proposing what? He refused to think about it.

"She's not my type," he told Clancy loudly. The hound was sitting by the door. Dave jumped up, feeling foolish and disoriented. Clancy's walk was the day's first chore, and it had gone clean out of his mind. He shook his head, hoping to clear it, then shrugged on his sheepskin coat and snapped Clancy's leash to his collar, taking refuge in the ordinary.

He thought about Rowen off and on all day. Every time he did, he made himself recall Karen's blue eyes and generous curves—and what she had cost him in time and effort, not to speak of cash. But the simple burden of supporting two people had not been the half of it.

"Leave it alone!" he ordered himself. Rowen had been sweet to take him to the play, but he had taken her to dinner. He figured they were even.

That evening he went out drinking, flying out of the apartment as though the devil himself might ring the phone.

He kept very busy the next morning, but drawing gave him too much time to think, even with the radio on. At noon he went out to buy groceries and get his mail. Among the bills he found an invitation to the opening of a show of paintings by a friend of his, a woman he had worked with. A handwritten line at the bottom invited him to a party afterward at her loft in Soho.

The gallery was on Madison Avenue. Near Rowen's shop. He sat at the drawing board and thought how easy it would be to pick her up after work, spend an hour at the opening, take her downtown to the party and deliver her to her door. No complications. His blood stirred at the thought of seeing her—her pretty face, her thin, delicate frame.

His hand tightened, putting so much pressure on his pencil that the lead broke. He flung the pencil on the floor, disgusted, and knew he was going to ask Rowen to go to the opening with him. He looked at the invitation again. It was for Thursday. Three days to wait.

He wanted to see her *now*. Well, not this minute. But tonight. He could get there before the shop closed and walk home with her. Invite her then. Maybe even coax her up for pizza. What happened after that would be . . . well, up to the gods. The thought of her delicate body stirred something within him. Maybe he'd only just discovered his type.

He found the shop without much trouble. It was small and narrow and crammed with books. Bookshelves that reached to the ceiling lined the perimeters of the room like some kind of crazy insulation. The books seemed uniformly gray-brown. Many of them were bound in crumbling leather.

And there was Rowen, behind a high counter in the back corner. Her wide dark eyes peered across a haphazard stack of oversize volumes. He wanted to laugh. He was so glad to see her, and she looked so funny and businesslike, such a pretty thing to be surrounded by crumbling, musty volumes. She looked pale, but it might be the light.

Rowen watched the man enter and wondered if her eyes were deluding her. She gripped the book she was pricing, wanting it to be Dave.

He came to the counter, his blue eyes bright and candid. She felt the blood stain her cheeks and seemed unable to look away.

Before he could speak someone came up to pay for a book, and Dave stepped back. She made change with trembling fingers.

"I was in the neighborhood," he said when she finished with the customer, "so I thought I'd drop in and walk you home . . . if you're going home."

"I . . . yes. Yes, I'm going home." She glanced at her watch, her thoughts whirling. She wanted to see him; she didn't want to see him. "I can't close for another fifteen minutes."

"I'll wait." His lips curved in a smile. "Where are the art books?"

She pointed to a section along the back wall, and he moved away.

She found it hard to behave naturally. She wanted to shout, "Hurray!" Then she remembered that the time spent with him would be another episode of skirting the truth. Of telling lies. Why hadn't she made up her mind how to tell him about herself if he asked her out again? She'd been afraid he wouldn't, then afraid he would. Only now was she beginning to get her mind away from the first huge mistake of her life. Why was she so eager to set forth on another disaster?

What made her think that she and Dave had met through some heavenly plan? More likely their attraction was a freaky chemical reaction that would dissipate as soon as they knew each other better.

It was still cold, wintry daylight a quarter of an hour later when they locked and barred the shop. Office workers were scurrying homeward. Rowen concentrated on keeping Vicky at her heels so the dog wouldn't get stepped on or tripped over.

"I got an invitation this morning," Dave began. "It's to an opening at a gallery near here. For Thursday. I wondered if you'd like to go."

Rowen dodged two pedestrians and heard herself say she would.

"Great!" Dave exclaimed. "There'll be a party afterward in Soho."

Rowen gulped. She hated parties where she knew no one, had, in fact, refused to go when she was married to Joe, but that was because Joe behaved so badly, drinking too much, flirting with all the women.

"I'm not much of a party person," she hedged.

"Do you think I am?" Dave grinned down at her, his blue eyes warm. He had taken her arm to keep them from being separated, and now she felt like pulling away. "If we don't like it, we'll leave."

With a sinking feeling Rowen realized that Dave might well like a party she hated. He was good-looking and outgoing. He'd be an asset in any crowd. Whereas she . . .

"I take it the artist having the show is a friend of yours?"

"Pauline Sanders. I worked with her at an ad agency. Listen, what are your plans for dinner?"

"Tonight?" Rowen asked in surprise. "I don't have any special plans," she said.

"That's what I figured," Dave said severely. "Listen, this

place down the street has the best pizza in New York. How about taking one to my place? I've got wine. Not as good as what you brought the other night, but . . ."

"We could take it to my house," Rowen offered. "There's wine there, too." In her own surroundings she would be forced to explain her circumstances, and the sooner she did that the better.

"My place is closer." Dave smiled. She let him have his way and took it as a reprieve.

Returning to Dave's apartment was like coming home. She looked forward to seeing the physical center of his life again. Despite the stark furnishings, she found his quarters both cozy and exciting. Like Dave himself.

He took her coat and gave Vicky a dog biscuit. Rowen cleared the coffee table while he poured the wine and set out plates.

They sat and feasted. When the slices of pizza cooled, Vicky and Clancy were allowed to share.

"What's better than this?" Dave demanded, sitting back with a deep breath of satisfaction. "Red wine and probably the best pizza in the world."

Rowen smiled. At the moment the differences in Dave's background and hers didn't trouble her belief that their lives were meant to intertwine. Little quirks only made the whole thing more amazing. Could two people from such different backgrounds fall in love? Definitely yes.

Could it last? That was the hitch. She had thought she was in love with Joe—at first. She had believed Joe when he said he loved her. What a mistake that had been!

"How come you never mention your folks?" Dave asked suddenly. "Where did you grow up?"

"In Connecticut—Old Lyme. My grandparents lived there. I don't talk about my parents because they died when I was a baby. They were on a luxury liner that sank off the coast of Long Island."

"I'm sorry." Dave put down his wineglass and took her hand in both of his. "You *are* a waif."

"I'm not!" She pulled her hand free. "I thoroughly enjoyed boarding school, and my grandparents spoiled me rotten." She frowned. "Except for money. They kept me on a strict allowance."

"Are they still alive?"

She shook her head. Her grandfather had died when she needed him most, when her marriage was coming apart. Both her grandparents had gone to their graves believing she had someone to take care of her.

"Are your parents alive?" she asked to change the subject. She often resented other people's relatives. When holidays came they took her friends away.

"Alive and well on a farm in southern Missouri. My youngest brother does most of the farming now. Dad hunts and fishes. Mom paints pictures to sell to the tourists. The farm's on the edge of the Ozarks. I have two older sisters and two younger brothers."

"The middle child."

"Yes, that's why I'm so easy-going."

"Are you?"

"Except when I get excited. Like now." He reached for her hand and tugged. "Come over here."

She let him pull her down beside him on the lumpy couch. "Rowen," he whispered. His arm tightened about her.

She closed her eyes, her happiness threatening to overflow. She loved the healthy male scent of him, blending with the laundry-soap smell of his cotton flannel shirt and the faint scent of ink, or perhaps lead pencils. . . . His hold tightened.

She raised her face, eager to lose herself in his drugging kisses. His tongue teased her lips, and then his mouth took hers hungrily. She relaxed in his arms, happy and trusting. He tasted of wine, yet sweeter. She responded with an eagerness new to her, and heard his husky voice.

"My God, Rowen. What is it you do? I just see you and I feel you belong to me. Or I belong to you. What happens when we come together?"

"I don't know," she murmured against his lips. She was unwilling to be the first to use the word *love*. She returned his kisses greedily, yet she longed to talk, too. She wanted to know everything about him.

"You knew I'd come looking for you, didn't you?" His deft fingers discovered that her dress was two pieces, separated at the waist. He slipped his hand beneath the fine wool and stroked her smooth silk undergarment. She sighed with satisfaction at the thought of him discovering that she wore a camisole and no bra. She struggled to concentrate on his question.

"After Vicky bit you?"

"Yes. I couldn't let you go out of my life." His mouth, his tongue, trailed down the side of her neck, emptying her mind of everything but the enjoyment she felt at his touch.

"No, I didn't expect to see you," she purred, her hands busy on their own, stroking the firm curves of his back, his shoulders, his biceps.

He turned her to face him. She felt his hands beneath her camisole, clasping the bare skin below her ribs. In a moment his fingers would slide up until his thumbs touched her breasts. She shivered in anticipation, her thoughts chaotic. It happened and the world reeled. His lips took hers possessively. His tongue drove deep into her mouth, promising delights still in store.

"I had to see you today," he murmured between kisses. She felt his breath on her lips. "You weren't surprised, were you? You must have known what I felt the other night when you came back with Mel. You knew it in the park, too. Didn't you?" he urged.

He moved his thumbs tantalizingly back and forth across her thrusting nipples until she gasped, her eyes closed, her mind open to anything he said or did.

"I knew," she answered.

"You're such a little thing," he marveled. "I never realized a woman could be so small, so pliant, so . . . fragile."

Rowen gazed up to find him smiling. His lips hovered tantalizingly close.

"You're used to strapping models with lots of flesh," she accused.

"Never again!" He kissed her deeply, holding her with one arm while his hand caressed her breast. She let herself be immersed in pure sensuality until a rattle of paper on the coffee table startled them both.

Dave raised his head. "Hey!" She felt as well as heard his shout.

Her eyes flew open to see Clancy tiptoeing away, a slice of pizza clamped between his teeth. Dave let Rowen go and she sat up reluctantly, biting her lip.

Dave pried the pizza from Clancy's jaws and returned to the couch laughing. He closed the box on the rescued slices. "I was planning to have that for breakfast."

He reached for Rowen, but she eluded his touch and stood up. The mood was broken, and she was glad. This was madness. How could she go looking for heartache again so soon? She wasn't ready for another commitment.

Dave accepted her decision, saying, "Come on, I'll walk you home."

"About Thursday," he mentioned, helping her into her coat. "You'll want to take Vicky home. I'll come by about six. There'll be food at the party, but maybe we'll stop on the way. You need a square meal."

"I wish you'd stop trying to fatten me up!" Rowen objected indignantly. "I'm not something you roast for Thanksgiving!"

"What makes you think I'm going to wait till Thanksgiving?" Dave leered.

When they were out on the street, their dogs trotting sedately alongside them, he suddenly asked, "What do you do for lunch? Do you eat?" His expression was no longer joking.

"Of course I eat!" Rowen said, incensed at his prying.

"What—a cup of yogurt?"

She smiled ruefully at his insight. That *was* often what she ate.

At her door he gathered her into his arms. Earlier feelings came rushing back, overwhelming them both.

"Dave . . ." Impulsively she wished they were back at his apartment.

He seemed to understand and hugged her tighter.

"Don't worry about a thing." He gave her a heart-stopping kiss and turned away.

On arriving home Thursday night she chose a gathered skirt of dark colors handwoven in Peru. She teamed it with a yellow cashmere sweater and a leather vest she had never worn. She hunted through her jewelry until she found an Indian necklace with a silver pendant and fat silver beads. The very thing!

She was waiting when the doorbell rang, and she called out to Pearl that she would answer it. She felt confident. Nothing could get very intense between her and Dave in the midst of a social situation, and afterward he could bring her home. She could invite him in . . . and tell him then.

The small gallery they went to was upstairs. The painter stood near the door. She was tall, her black hair streaked with gray. She wore black pants, an intricately knitted sweater and dangling earrings. Dave hugged and congratulated her and introduced Rowen.

Before they had exchanged more than two sentences, more people arrived. Dave steered Rowen toward a table bearing a vase of flowers and a guest book. At the other end were glasses of champagne.

Rowen didn't sign the guest book. The gallery manager would be excited to see her Sutton Place address, and why raise false hopes?

They helped themselves to champagne. Before they could look at the paintings, Dave was drawn into conversation by one person and then another. Each time he introduced Rowen, but she was content to stand back, watching Dave and the warmth with which acquaintances greeted him.

"You know a lot of the people here," she remarked when they were alone for a minute.

"They're advertising types. Pauline and I worked for the same agencies. And I've been to parties at her loft before."

Rowen was stricken by the primitive emotion that washed over her. Two very attractive women claimed Dave's attention, giving her a chance to recover her balance. She wandered away, leaving the two women in temporary possession.

She tried to inspect the artwork, but the rooms were crowded. She liked the painter's style. The works were small, intricate still lifes with lots of pleasing color. She realized she could buy one if she chose.

When she returned to Dave, he was talking to two other people. He tucked her hand under his arm and smiled down at her, making her breath catch. "I don't know about you, but I'm hungry. Are you ready to go?"

Rowen indicated that she was.

"How'd you like Pauline's work?" Dave asked when they were outside and walking toward the subway. "Some people say it's too feminine—"

"Men, I suppose! What if it is? Anyhow, I did like it. Maybe I'll go back and see the show one day when there isn't such a crowd. I wouldn't mind buying one."

"Her prices are pretty stiff. I don't know what you were thinking of spending. . . ."

"I don't know, either," Rowen said quickly. "It was just an idea."

Dave flung his arm around her. "One opening and she's an art collector."

Rowen laughed and then frowned, puzzled. "Wasn't that why people were invited—to buy?"

"Not people like us!"

"Oh," Rowen said in a small voice.

They took a subway to Soho and found a small Italian restaurant with booths along one wall. They sat across the table from each other. Dave took her hands and looked deeply into her eyes.

"I love being with you," he said simply.

But when the waiter came, he insisted on ordering hearty plates of spaghetti and meatballs, promising Rowen that she needed to eat only what she felt comfortable with.

They laid aside the menus, and she folded her arms across her chest, shielding herself. If Dave found her skinny and unattractive, why had he bothered to invite her out? She dreaded the party. Dave, with his relaxed, good-natured personality, would be popular with everyone. She would be left standing on the sidelines with a smile pasted on her face. Why hadn't she had enough sense to stay with her own crowd, where people were friendly because she was one of them? They all had money or expectations, except for chiselers like Joe. Dave, in fact, was one of the few people she knew who didn't have money.

Dave noticed her silence. "You're very quiet."

"I'm tired of being pushed to eat." She added waspishly, "If you don't like the way I look, you don't have to ask me out."

"Aw, honey! I love being with you. I mean it!" Dave reached out to cup her face. His eyes searched hers with an intensity that stirred her uncomfortably. "I won't say another thing! I think you're beautiful—even when you're pouting."

He leaned his forearms on the table and captured her hands again. "I have this primitive need to take care of . . . people. I fight it all the time." He grinned and sat back as the waiter arrived with their food.

Rowen picked up her fork with a sense of loss. She didn't seem to know *what* she wanted—a man who would let her alone or one who would fuss over her. She told herself not to be silly. Women didn't need to be taken care of any more than men did. On the other hand, she rather liked it.

She let her gaze rest warmly on Dave as he tackled the spaghetti. It would be fun to look after him, too. In little ways—sharing his satisfaction when he sold a cartoon, consoling him when he got rejections, as she supposed he must. She could help him financially, if he'd let her, though he seemed to have everything he needed.

She smiled up at him. "I'll forgive you this time."

They finished the meal amicably. Rowen ate more than she really wanted because it was so delicious.

They were fashionably late by the time they reached the building where Pauline lived.

"I suppose you've been to lofts before," Dave said, opening one of the double doors that led off the street. Rowen saw wide, dimly lit stairs going straight up, flight beyond flight, like a ladder to heaven.

"I went to a party in one once. The host was a wealthy filmmaker. The interior decorator had put in a sauna."

"Pauline's isn't like that! In fact, it's pretty basic."

The sounds of the party led them up the stairs and through an open door. The floor-through space was filled with people. Most were standing in groups, talking and drinking. Up near the front windows some couples were dancing.

Rowen looked in wonder at the high, pressed-tin ceiling. Walls, floor and ceiling were painted white. Dave hung their coats on an iron rack, then led Rowen through the crowd to a table at the back, where refreshments were set out.

"First wine and then Pauline," he said with a laugh.

Rowen relaxed a bit. Dave filled plastic glasses with wine and stood beside her, looking over the crowd.

"I must know a few people here," he muttered. "Anyway, this is Pauline's loft. Not bad, for the rent she pays."

"Where does she sleep and keep her clothes?" Rowen looked about. The huge room, which had windows at either end, seemed almost empty, the few pieces of furniture lost in the vast space.

"Most of these places have a sleeping platform built in. It leaves more space for the studio. You can read up there or watch TV. They use the underneath for a dressing room. Platforms are warmer, too, being closer to the ceiling. These places are hard to heat."

"I notice!"

"Are you cold?" Dave's instant concern threw her off-balance. She hadn't meant to complain. She wanted to see his world.

"Not really." She repressed a shiver, unsure whether it came from cold or nervousness.

"Drink up, and I'll get you more wine. That'll warm you."

She let him take her glass and refill it.

"Would you like to have a loft?" she asked when he returned.

"My place is okay for my kind of work," he said, but Rowen thought she detected a wistful note in his voice.

They said hello again to Pauline, and then stood watching the other guests. Dave's party spirit was almost tangible. It burst out when three men descended on him, radiating wine and goodwill.

Dave grinned and introduced Rowen. They smiled politely but soon crowded around him. Obviously he was popular.

"Hey, come on. I want some people over here to meet you." One, who was bald and chubby, grasped Dave's arm and urged him into the crowd.

Dave threw Rowen a laughing look over his shoulder. "I'll be right back," he shouted above the tumult.

She laughed back, happy to see him sought after despite being left alone herself. "Go ahead. I'll be all right."

He went off with a zest she admired and envied.

All her lessons in poise and making gracious small talk had never taught her to enjoy large gatherings full of strangers. She felt more comfortable on the fringe, listening. Then, if the conversation was boring, she could move on. She pasted a smile on her face and eavesdropped on the nearest chattering group.

No one stopped to talk to her. They could probably tell that she didn't fit in. She probably looked too uptight. This was the kind of crowd Dave knew—talented people who had come to New York from all over. She began to feel skinny and undesirable and stupid, unworthy of being liked for herself.

She looked for a place to sit where she wouldn't be obviously alone. Two people abandoned one end of a long bench, and she arrived at it just as a man with a black beard and bright black eyes approached from the opposite direction.

"Don't I know you from somewhere?" the man began as they both sat down.

Rowen managed a wintry smile. "Not unless you're into rare books. I run a bookshop uptown."

"Ah!" To her surprise he named the bookstore. "I never forget a pretty face." His eyes narrowed in a smile, and his beard parted to reveal white teeth. "That's the oldest approach in the world, but this time it's true. I've collected the complete works of Robert Louis Stevenson, mostly from your shop."

His name was Theo. They chatted awhile, and then he surprised her by saying, "They're dancing up front. Would you care to dance?"

She was in Theo's arms, dancing to something lively, when she caught sight of Dave arguing heatedly with two men and a woman. He looked up, as though the mysterious connection between him and Rowen alerted him to her nearness. Before the movement of the dance hid him from view, she saw his blue eyes widen. He cocked his head in surprise, as if to say, "I thought I left you against the wall!"

Rowen dropped her head into Theo's shoulder to hide an impish smile. How would Dave react?

As the music ended, he materialized at her side with gratifying promptness. "My dance, I think," he told Theo. He slipped his arm about Rowen's waist and swung her into the rhythm of the next tune.

She watched his face doubtfully, wondering if he would be angry. His mouth was unsmiling, and she caught a blaze in his blue eyes, but it was quickly hidden when he turned his head away.

She placed her hand lightly on his shoulder, aware of the powerful muscles beneath his blue wool shirt, and a wave of excitement engulfed her. She had felt the same thrill when he had held her before, but this time it was heightened by his flattering possessiveness.

"You didn't lose much time," he commented at last. He kept his voice casual, but the spark of fire in his glance told another story.

"No, I didn't." She smiled serenely. "That man turned out to be a customer of the bookstore. What happened to your argument?"

"Oh, that!" Dave's brow cleared, and his laugh rang out. He again became the easygoing man she knew. "I don't even remember what we were talking about. The minute I saw you in that guy's arms, I lost interest. It was as bad as seeing Clancy walk off with some stranger!"

"Are you comparing me to your hound?" she cried with mock affront.

"I love my hound," he said, pulling her tight against his chest.

Her cheek was against the soft front of his shirt. Underneath, he felt as hard and solid as a barrel. The way he was holding her made a reply impossible. She was glad of that. The wine seemed to have confused her. Did Dave mean he loved her, too? It wasn't her money; he didn't know about that!

Dave's thoughts were whirling. This skinny little woman had become very precious to him, and to hell with all his plans for being independent. He wanted to make love to her—tonight. Deliberately he closed his mind against rational thought. He had known for days that this desire would get the better of him. Why resist—if she was willing?

"Let's get out of here," he urged, his voice husky. "Okay?" Before she could answer, he had swept her through the crowd, into her coat, and downstairs. At the cross street he hailed a taxi.

In the backseat he pulled her close against him. He gave the driver the address of his apartment, and Rowen made no protest. She scarcely had time to draw a surprised breath before his lips found hers and she drifted into a world bounded by strong, loving arms, where she was kept in orbit by kisses. Pressed against his sheepskin coat as she was, she could feel the strong thumping of his heart.

"What am I going to do with you?" he muttered.

"Kiss me again."

"I knew I had something in mind!" he quipped, and complied with her request.

5

﹏﹏﹏﹏

At Dave's building they walked wordlessly up the stairs, as though their bodies had reached an agreement their minds were not a party to. She waited, breathless and frightened, while Dave unlocked his door and flipped the light switch. Clancy sprawled near the drawing table. His tail thumped the floor in welcome.

"He's too lazy to get up," Dave said. After stripping off Rowen's coat and his own, he led her into the bedroom. "Come in here where I can kiss you."

"You have kissed me," she whispered, suddenly wishing she had made him take her home. How many times had she promised herself that she would be cautious about getting involved again? And then this irresistible attraction had flashed between them.

"I haven't kissed you the way I intend to." He picked her up and laid her on the mattress. He knelt beside the bed, touching a dark tendril that curled against the alabaster skin of her neck before burying his face in her hair. In silence the tension between them built.

"I should warn you," she said at last, needing to hear his voice. "I'm not voluptuous."

She felt the warm breath from his explosion of intimate laughter. "But you're very amusing," he said tenderly, his lips brushing her ear, his words a caress. "You please me just the way you are."

She sighed with anticipation as his cool fingertips traced the outline of her jaw before he turned her face to meet his lips.

He claimed her mouth with a kiss that thrilled her to the quick and sent her over the edge into a country that was all feeling, all sensuality. Dave and she were meant to be a part of each other; in her bones she knew it with no hint of doubt.

All the earlier part of the evening had been leading to this. Her lips parted. The tip of his tongue traced their contours before invading her mouth to touch and tantalize. She responded with little sounds of pleasure. Her tongue met his, teasing, tasting, tormenting. Her breath came faster; her blood grew hotter. His hands stroked her face, her ears, her hair. Never had she known that lovemaking could be so wonderful, so sweeping.

She had never felt so thrillingly alive, and at the same time so languorous. A glow came from the street, lighting the planes of Dave's face, making deep hollows of his eyes until he looked like a stranger, but his touch and his unique masculine scent were burningly familiar.

Lying on her back on the puffy quilt, Rowen delighted in the coziness—two people adrift on a sea of feelings. The room was warm, and Dave had closed the door, so nothing would interrupt them. She slid her fingers through his unruly hair. She traced the laugh lines at the corner of his eye and gloried in the slight, masculine roughness of his jawline.

She felt his body tremble and realized that he, too, was fired with expectation. At this moment he wanted her as a woman. He knew nothing about her background. Nothing! He wanted her for herself. She aroused him, made him tremble. When they were together, lightning flashed between them.

She brought his hand to her lips, kissing his fingertips while she lifted heavy eyelids to stare up at him in wonder.

"Rowen," he breathed, his voice husky. "Oh, Rowen!"

Her name on his lips was a cry of worship. The blue-black depths of his eyes reflected the streetlight. She felt the give of the mattress as he stretched beside her—long, male, solid.

His body half covered hers as their kisses grew more intense. A series of tremors raced through her. She felt the pressure of his manhood against her side and was swept by the tumultuous knowledge that it was meant for her.

She found herself growing short of breath as the kiss went on and on, and she moaned softly in reaction. Dave raised his head. Twining her fingers in his thick locks, she drew his mouth fiercely back to hers.

"Dave," she gasped, her voice a cry of pleading.

He seemed to know what she meant, and the demand added fuel to his urgency. She felt him unbuckle his belt and a second later heard him fling his trousers to the floor while his mouth held hers captive.

"Rowen, I want you as I've never wanted anything." His voice was deep with emotion. "I wanted you from the minute I saw you, I think. My brain was slower than my body, that's all. When I saw you dancing with that guy tonight . . ." He laughed shakily. "I realized that I already considered you mine. Does that make me some kind of barbarian? Believe me, I felt pretty primitive."

His hand slipped beneath her sweater. Without ending the drugging kiss, he used both hands to pull her sweater higher. His fingers found the triangle of bare skin above her camisole. He bent his head and darted his tongue to taste the pale cleft between her breasts.

"Sit up and let me look at you," he coaxed.

Willingly she sat up. Dave followed and pulled her sweater over her head. He flung it away and slid capable hands down the satin camisole, pulling the shiny cloth taut across her breasts.

"Beautiful!" he murmured. "Where'd I get the idea you were skinny? Do you realize I almost never see you when you aren't muffled to the eyebrows? Down coats, long-sleeved sweaters . . ." He broke off to touch the thrusting tip of her breast with a teasing forefinger, making her gasp. He recaptured her mouth with his own as his hand slid beneath the satin to the silkiness of her thrusting flesh.

"I want to touch you, too," she breathed, struggling with the buttons of his shirt.

He peeled off his shirt in a swift motion that made her smile. "Touch me—I'm all yours." His rough-and-ready style amused her only for an instant. Then his hands stripped her of her camisole. Her breath caught in her throat as his lips captured one swelling breast and then the other.

Rowen encountered the firm flesh and unyielding bone of his hips as her hands sought the throbbing shape of him. Between kisses they discarded the rest of their clothes until they lay naked on the red-brown quilt. Rowen sensed hunger in Dave's devouring kisses. Her body surged to reply with a hunger of her own.

He gathered her against the long lines of his powerful frame. She felt faint with greedy anticipation. One arm wrapped her waist, while his other hand clutched her rounded buttocks as she arched against him.

Her hands slid over his flesh, enjoying a sensual exploration of their own as Dave's skillful touch brought her passion higher and ever higher.

"Dave, please, please!"

Such a pitch of desire was new to her. She had believed herself incapable of wild arousal, but now she cried out for his strong thrust to make them one.

When it did, she gasped with pure delight. Dave held them still for a long moment before taking her up and up to the secret shrine sacred only to feeling.

They reached it, invaded it, and her flaming response sent them both into a realm of pure pleasure.

They floated down from the heights, unable to do more than hold each other while passion receded, leaving in its wake a glorious belonging—to each other, to life.

"Rowen," Dave groaned at last, his head on her breast. "You have a beautiful body."

He rose above her, supporting his weight on taut arms, and looked her up and down. She looked him over with equal candor, admiring his broad forearms and the interesting line of hair that made a little path down the middle of him. She closed her eyes, not wanting to see him leave her.

He went to the kitchen and poured two glasses of wine and brought them back to the bedroom.

"It's getting cold in here!" He shivered and covered her with the quilt before sliding in beside her.

Curled against him, she fell asleep. She still hadn't told him about herself. She had promised herself that she would do it this evening. But when had she had a chance?

She woke in the middle of the night to the thrilling touch of his fingers on her breasts. Heat shot through her instantly. He hovered over her, and she drew him in, delighting in his arousal.

They slept again, their physical desire temporarily sated. Dave held her hand. Lovers should lie in each other's arms, Rowen thought drowsily, but she was content with this beginning.

When she next woke, it was to the clear light of morning. Dave should have been beside her. Instead, his side of the bed was empty. She heard the click of Clancy's nails on the bare floor outside the bedroom and caught a whiff of coffee.

It was indeed morning, and she was assailed with doubt. And guilt. She shouldn't have let last night happen. She had fallen in love with a man who didn't even know the real Rowen Hill. She was a stranger to him, someone he might treat quite differently when he knew the truth about her. She already knew him well enough to know he would be angry when he learned that she'd lied to him. Not lied, exactly, but . . . dissembled, wasn't that the word? She had skirted the truth, let him think his guesses were correct, that his intuition was right instead of dead wrong.

She had planned to have Dave take her straight home from the party, and that was the way the evening would have turned out if that man Theo hadn't danced with her. Dave's jealousy had aroused his desire. It was as simple as that.

"Black, right?" Dave broke into her unwelcome thoughts, appearing at the bedroom door with two steaming cups.

Rowen watched as he set the cups on the sturdy tables on either side of the bed. She ached to smooth his tousled hair. He had pulled on the bottoms of a pair of blue cotton flannel pajamas, leaving his well-muscled chest and shoulders bare. The air in the apartment was icy. Rowen shivered, conscious of her nakedness.

"Here . . ." He handed her the matching top, and she cringed, pulling the sheet up to her neck. He didn't want to see pert, thrusting breasts. He would have preferred the overflowing bosoms one saw on nudes in paintings. Shyly, hopefully, she raised her face for a kiss. His lips barely touched her cheek.

She shrank back against the pillows he piled behind her and searched his face while he tucked the down quilt around her shoulders. He looked unusually solemn. She watched him walk around the bed and pull a thick sweatshirt over his torso.

"Do Missouri boys chop wood to get such muscles?" she asked, trying to lighten the heavy silence.

"This one did." He didn't smile. He sat cross-legged on the bed, facing her. "We have to talk."

Rowen's stomach dropped. She had sensed that something unpleasant was coming.

"What do we have to talk about?" she made herself ask.

"Me . . . You . . . Us."

"Us? What makes you think there *is* an us?" she demanded, taking refuge in being the first to deny it.

He looked at her, his blue eyes steady. "You know there is."

She bit her lip, refusing to meet his gaze. "What, then?"

"I shouldn't have brought you here last night. I shouldn't

even have taken you out!" He ran a shaking hand through his light brown hair. "Damn it, I can't *afford* to feel about a woman the way I feel about you!"

"What do you mean?"

He ran his hand through his hair again. "I don't want to take life so seriously. I don't want to be responsible for another person's happiness. What I mean is"—he shrugged, avoiding her eyes—"I don't want to settle down to one woman. Get involved. That's the current word, isn't it? *Involved?*" His handsome mouth twisted.

"How are we involved?"

"How? After last night you can ask me how?"

A careless shrug, a taunting smile, implied that she could ask, and *was.*

Dave's eyes widened, then narrowed. "Don't tell me that last night wasn't overwhelming for you, too! That was no act you were putting on."

Rowen was torn between salvaging her pride and being honest. Honesty won. It was time she stopped giving Dave wrong impressions. The bond between them was too important.

"All right," she agreed. "Last night *was* important. It was wonderful. So how can you turn away from it this morning?"

He stood up and strode to the window. "I know myself, Rowen. I don't want the emotional drain of having someone's happiness depending on me. Sometimes if I'm busy I don't answer my phone. I know women! They start wanting to know where you were, why you didn't answer, who you were out with—or in bed with. Or I get a desperate call from some ad agency, wanting me to work all night. I don't want to clear my comings and goings with *anyone!*"

"And you think that would be necessary?"

"Yes! I couldn't stand hurting you—your big brown eyes looking accusing. Like they are right now, if you want to know the truth! It isn't in me to hurt people, Rowen. I'd do it, not meaning to. It's better not to start."

"You really don't think we could work something out?"

"No." He folded his arms across his chest and continued to stare out the window.

The flat, uncompromising answer infuriated her. "I see," she said coolly. "Well, thanks for the roll in the hay. . . ." Her heart thudded so heavily that she was sure he would hear it.

Dave turned at last. "Don't put it that way. . . ." The look in his eyes struck her as oddly hurt.

"Sorry, does that make you homesick for Missouri?" Why should he look pained when she was the one being hurt, and he was the one doing the hurting? She jumped briskly out of bed. "May I have the bathroom first, since I have to go to work?"

She thought with sudden longing of Vicky. If she took a taxi, there would be time to go home and get the one creature who loved her.

In the stark bathroom the air was cold. Against her bare feet the black-and-white tile floor and the white bathtub were freezing. Her teeth chattered uncontrollably while she stripped Dave's pajama top from her slim body, her brown eyes wide with pain. What chilled her as much as the room was Dave's rejection. Without money, no one wanted her.

Luckily the water was hot. In the shower, she should have reveled in the memory of the way Dave had made love to her. Instead, his statement in the cold light of dawn drummed in her ears.

While the water played on her back, her mind ran furiously over his words. What a morning after! Now that he'd made love to her, he couldn't be bothered with her. That was what it amounted to. At least she hadn't cried aloud last night that she loved him.

But when she considered it, his behavior was inconsistent. It didn't jibe with the other things she knew about him. A man who liked animals wasn't a man who thought only of himself. *I can't afford to feel about a woman the way I feel about you.* The phrase echoed in her head. Could he have meant it literally—that he feared she'd be a financial burden? Recalling how often he'd called her a waif, she thought perhaps he *had*

76

meant it literally, and that he'd been too proud to spell it out. Suddenly the outlook brightened. She'd better tell him the truth. He'd change his mind then, all right, she concluded cynically.

She stepped out of the shower and began to dress, her thoughts dwelling grimly on how surprised he'd be. . . .

Dave continued to stand at the bedroom window, looking down at the traffic, listening to the shower run. When it stopped, he swallowed the lump in his throat and with a sigh returned to the kitchen. He'd make her a good breakfast before she left.

He stood in the kitchen and stared into space. He had tried to make the break as painless as possible for her. She was dismayed now by his apparent lack of character, but after a day or two she'd shrug her shoulders. She'd dismiss him as just another New York bastard looking out for *numero uno*.

Maybe he should have told her the truth, repeated what he'd said the first time she came to dinner: that he couldn't afford to marry. Wouldn't. Wouldn't take a full-time job for any woman, not even Rowen.

Just now he'd been too vain to tell her that financially he couldn't afford an emotional entanglement. It wasn't fair to ask a woman to live from hand to mouth the way he did. And nothing in the forseeable future was going to make cartooning anything but a day-to-day gamble.

Yet he knew himself. He'd want to spend money on Rowen. He'd want to watch her eyes light up the way they had when he invited her to the gallery opening. Damn it, he liked to spend money on women as much as the next guy. He'd want to buy her things, and you had to make choices in life.

Maybe, sometime, he'd meet a woman who could afford to carry her share of the financial burden, and if his career kept going well, they could team up. But this woman was too gentle, too sweet. Too dependent. That was the bottom line.

Rowen came out of the bathroom, dressed and defiant. Anger, hurt and a certain amount of guilt warred in her breast. Dave called from the kitchen, and she marched in, ready to tell him what he was losing. The sight of two places laid on the small Formica-topped table disarmed her.

"Sit down," he ordered gruffly. "You're not leaving without a decent breakfast."

He was behaving just as though he hadn't dismissed her, hadn't told her to get out of his life. At a loss for words, she sat. Dave filled her coffee cup.

"Eggs and toast coming up," he announced. An instant later, with a loud click, the toaster tossed two slices onto the table. Rowen jumped.

Dave grunted. "One of those bank gifts. A friend passed it on."

What friend? Rowen wondered jealously. As she had dressed in the steamy bathroom, she had tried without success to frame a quick confession that she could deliver curtly on her way out. Now, over breakfast, she could explain slowly. It seemed important to make Dave understand why she had let him imagine that she was—what had he called her—a poor little match girl.

Dave served up the scrambled eggs and joined her at the table.

Rowen picked up her fork and let her eyes roam over him. How she loved his looks—his candid blue eyes and unruly light brown hair, the humorous set of his sensitive mouth, though just now it formed a straight, determined line. She drew a deep, painful breath. He still had his night's growth of beard because she'd monopolized the bathroom. Her heart thudded.

She laid her fork down again and took a sip of coffee.

His eyes met hers over the cup. "Is something wrong with the eggs?"

"No, nothing. But there's something I think I should tell you. Before we part," she added, cynicism tinging her voice.

"Can't you eat while you talk?"

"I don't think I can eat at all," she said with a trace of childish malice. "The fact is, Dave . . . I haven't been quite honest with you. You assumed things, and I let you—"

"Don't tell me you're married!"

She gave a bitter smile. "What difference would it make? Since everything's over anyhow."

He reached across the table and grabbed her wrist. She knew at once that she wanted nothing so much as for him to pull her to her feet and against his chest.

"Are you married? Don't lie to me!" His expression was fierce.

"No, I'm not!" she said hastily. "I'm talking about money." She had his full attention now and hoped that her words would throw him as much as she'd been thrown by his determination not to see her again. "For some reason you've insisted on thinking I'm hard up. The truth is, I have . . ."

Suddenly the oft-repeated advice of her grandfather flashed into her mind. *Never admit you have a dime. If you do, people will try to take it away from you.* When her marriage had ended so disastrously, she had sometimes wished that Joe had succeeded. But she hadn't wished that recently. This morning the fact that she had money was giving her a lot of satisfaction. She was going to let Dave know just how much he'd thrown over.

"The truth is?" Dave prompted.

Rowen took another sip of coffee. Her grandfather's advice won out. She didn't need to tell him exactly how much she had.

"Lack of money is not my problem," she stated. "I have a very nice trust fund. Furthermore, I'm not just a clerk at that bookstore. I own half of it, and I'm learning the business so eventually I can run the place alone."

Dave clenched his fork, his shoulders rigid. Very slowly a tide of red crept up his neck to suffuse his cheeks. His mouth became a straight, angry line. "You lied to me!"

"No! I can't help what you assumed!"

"You let me worry about you, thinking that you were hard up and not eating enough!"

"How could anyone living on Sutton Place not be getting enough to eat?" she jibed.

"But you looked—" He glared at her. "You always look like you need taking care of."

"I do not! You only imagine I do. You wanted to think so, and I let you."

He pushed his plate away, his eggs half eaten. She would never have thought his eyes could look so cold. "Why are you telling me this now?"

She shrugged, a pretense of callousness. "I thought you should know your intuition doesn't work as well as you think." She certainly wasn't going to lay it on the line for him that she wouldn't be a drain on his finances. He'd have to work that out for himself. She wasn't sure if that was his reason for dumping her, and pain made her cautious.

"Are you house-sitting, or was that a lie, too?" he gritted.

"I wasn't obliged to tell you the house belongs to my aunt and uncle."

"I should have guessed," he muttered. "People don't go off and leave Sutton Place houses in the hands of strangers."

"So you can't exactly call me a waif, can you?" she pressed.

He jumped to his feet and stomped around the small kitchen. Finally, he turned to stare at her, his glare assessing. "At least I was honest with you. It may have hurt, but I gave it to you straight. I wasn't devious."

Rowen found that she couldn't meet his look. She remembered that her reason for telling him the truth had not been to make him mad and somehow get even for what he'd said that morning. The reason was that he deserved to know who she really was. He was right; he had been honest with her.

When she brought herself to face him, his expression had softened. He shook his head in puzzlement. "You still look like you need taking care of! But I guess that's my hang-up."

Rowen's heart sank. He hadn't been talking about finances, then. He wanted to go it alone emotionally, too.

She stood up, chin high. "I mustn't be late opening the shop."

"At least you don't have to worry about getting fired," he joked weakly.

"Is this good-bye?" she couldn't keep from asking at the door.

His reply was to order her to take care of herself. He took her chin in his hand and kissed her softly on the mouth.

She was too proud to cry on the way downstairs, but in the taxi she weakened momentarily and let the tears come. It was impossible not to recall the phrase "poor little rich girl," but the idea was so maudlin that she blew her nose and wiped her eyes. Dave's the one who should be crying, she told herself. Look at all the lovely money he's passing up.

At his drawing board Dave remembered the unfinished sketch he had done of Rowen and hunted through the drawings of Vicky until he found it. He studied the lines and shook his head. He hadn't even begun to catch her likeness.

He wadded it up, threw it in his wastebasket and filled his technical fountain pen. Then he laid it down and retrieved the drawing. He smoothed it out and pinned it to his bulletin board. It was all he had of her now.

He kept from thinking about her all weekend, as if his mind were numb. Monday morning, however, when he sat down to work, she leapt into his mind with the persistence of a hungry kitten, and there she stayed.

He tried to keep his anger simmering over the way she had deluded him, but it didn't work. No matter how hard he concentrated on what he was drawing, she sneaked into his consciousness—her face, her lips, her breasts, her voice, her scent—until he threw down his pencil in disgust. At lunchtime he caught himself wondering if she were eating properly.

"I really am off my rocker," he told Clancy.

It was after lunch that the insidious thought first crept in: If she's got so much money, I wouldn't have to feel financially responsible. *She's* the woman I was dreaming of who could pay her own way.

The idea seemed incredible. He simply couldn't think of Rowen as financially independent. He spent the afternoon telling himself she didn't need him. At about four o'clock he gave up.

"I don't care how much money she's got!" he told Clancy belligerently. "I still want to take care of her! And if she can support herself, it would be a lot easier."

He stalked to the telephone and dialed the bookshop, too eager to hear her voice to take time to think out an apology.

6

There were hours when Rowen could banish Dave from her thoughts, but he always turned up again. How could she have been so foolish—leaving herself open to hurt again? This time the pain was far worse than what she had felt when her marriage broke up. She would remember the way attraction crackled between them, and she would begin to hope.

His call came during one of the hopeful moments.

"Rowen? It's Dave. Don't hang up!"

Her throat tightened until she could barely speak. She hadn't known how wildly she'd been longing to hear that faintly midwestern accent and the caressing tone with which he always addressed her.

"I won't." Her words came out in a croak. A spasm of fear followed the initial joyous thrill. What did he want? She mustn't expect anything.

"Rowen, I haven't been able to stop thinking about you since you left the other morning. Was I a complete and total idiot? Could you possibly forgive me?"

"Forgive you for what?" she asked coolly. "For telling me the truth about yourself?"

"Yes, but . . ."

He paused for a long time. "What I told you the other morning wasn't exactly the truth—not the whole truth, anyway. Damn it, I should have planned this speech before I called! But I wanted to hear your voice . . . to know you were all right. Listen, maybe I should call back. Better yet, I'll meet you there after work—"

"No, don't do that!" she interrupted. She caught her breath. She couldn't bear to have him hang up before she heard what he had to say. "I'm not busy. We can talk now."

"Okay." He sighed. "I'd much rather be looking at you, but I guess you've got a right to hold me at arm's length. You're going to think I'm crazy, but the truth is . . ." He paused. "All those great principles I was talking about . . . today they don't seem to matter. Not when I weigh them against never seeing you again."

"And tomorrow?"

"Tomorrow they won't matter either. I know this is going to sound really crass, but if I don't have to be responsible for you financially, you do fit into my life."

"I see." She kept the comment unemotional, but her spirits went zinging up like a skylark.

He said, "I know how it sounds, like all I'm thinking about is the fact that you've got some money of your own, but . . . hell, I'm never going to be a steady provider, Rowen. Facts are facts. The other morning I figured it was better to let you down before we got in too deep."

"What about everything else you said?" she asked cautiously.

"Like what?"

Resentment rose in her. "That you didn't want to take life so seriously! That I'd make demands—want to know where you were when you didn't answer your phone, or if you didn't come home one night. Naturally I'd want to know! If someone is important to me, I want to know where he is. Don't you?"

"Of course I do," Dave agreed. "Rowen, I didn't mean half the stuff I said. I was running scared. I'm sorry, but I couldn't help it—I feel that I want to be looking after you. I care so much about your happiness. That morning my feelings were too much. I couldn't cope with them." He laughed shakily. "I'm not sure I can now, but I don't have any choice. The feelings go on whether I see you or not. *Are* you all right, by the way?"

"Yes, of course, I'm all right." She couldn't keep the lilt from her voice.

"Listen, I'll come around and meet you at closing time. We need to talk face-to-face. We can come back here, and I'll cook something."

"Oh, Dave, I can't tonight." Rowen clutched the phone, rigid with disappointment. "I've made plans for this evening." Despite her regrets her heart was soaring. He wasn't lukewarm about seeing her.

"Tomorrow night, then," he urged. "We can go out to dinner."

His eagerness touched her, made her feel cherished again. Then the imp in her brain, quite separate from her sentimental self, jeered, *Does he think you'll pay for it?*

Dave was too sincere to do anything so unworthy. She longed to be in the shelter of his arms right that moment.

He *was* sincere, wasn't he? Surely her attraction now wasn't her trust fund. The idea made her stiffen. She had to be wary this time around. Surely she was sophisticated enough now to be able to tell when a man was after her money. Dave *had* liked her before he knew.

He liked you so much he dumped you, the imp reminded her.

"Dave, I think you should come to my place," she said. That was the answer! She would show him her world and watch his behavior carefully. She would try to judge him objectively. His actions when he saw her in her natural surroundings would tell her something. She couldn't imagine him showing a greedy interest, but the test would be interesting.

He might feel out of place and back off. How would she feel about that?

Before she could follow that thought, Dave said, "Honey, you won't want to cook when you get home."

"The housekeeper does the cooking," she said airily.

"Oh. All right. Tomorrow night at seven, then. I can't wait."

It was raining the next evening when Rowen hurried home from work. She hung her raincoat in the hall and checked the dining room. The table was set for two. The sparkling glasses and shining silver made a welcome contrast to the wet, chilly outdoors. Pearl's seafood casserole, a variation of *coquille St. Jacques,* bubbled in the oven. The pink rosebuds and baby's breath in the cut-glass vase on the table were one of the expensive bouquets delivered regularly by her aunt's florist.

Rowen changed into very full silk lounging pajamas of her favorite ruby red. Two bottles of excellent white wine from her uncle's cellar were chilling in the refrigerator. Celia wouldn't be home until late, and Pearl had disappeared into her own small sitting room. With everything in readiness, Rowen poured herself a sherry and waited.

Dave arrived on time. At the sight of him, all Rowen's resentment fled. By trying to break off their relationship he had done what he thought was best. His pride wouldn't let him offer a woman less than what he thought she deserved.

"I brought Clancy." His words tumbled out while his guileless blue eyes ran over her, checking her from head to foot as though she were something precious he'd lost and then found again.

The hound took a step forward. That seemed to bring Dave's thoughts back to what he'd started to say. "Clancy has been acting strange—nervous—all day. He's not wet—I took a cab. I hope you don't mind. . . ."

"Of course not!"

Their eyes met. Wordlessly, hypnotized, they feasted on each other. Clancy dropped to the floor in his usual lazy-hound pose.

"Dave . . ."

"Rowen . . ."

Dave set aside the paper-wrapped wine bottle he carried and tore off his jacket. Then he swept her into his arms, holding her as though he'd been away two years. He was wearing a dark green sweater she hadn't seen before. The sight of it made her throat ache. They were such strangers! She didn't even know his clothes. His girl friend would have known. What was her name? Karen.

Dave's kiss started out gentle, then grew more and more heated. She molded herself against him. Every moment in his arms was important, to show him that she wanted him, too. Her blood was in flames when he loosed her, shaking his head in disbelief.

"I feel helpless . . . When I see you, I feel helpless."

"Come and have a glass of wine," she coaxed breathlessly, delighted that he, too, felt the force which drew them together. "Maybe wine will give you strength."

"Strength has nothing to do with it."

She turned from hanging his coat in the closet, and he caught her to him with a groan. "I love to touch you, to see you, to hear your voice . . . ." He buried his nose in her hair. "I love to smell you and taste you." She held her breath, hoping he might say, "I love *you.*" Instead she felt his teeth on her neck. A small shriek escaped her. Dave stepped back with a reluctant grin.

"Do you think I'm crazy?"

"Isn't that what a cartoonist needs to be?"

"Not this kind of—" He broke off. She had led him into the sitting room. He looked around in silence, taking in the air of expensive elegance. "Am I supposed to sit down?" he asked after a moment.

Rowen looked at him, unsure if he was joking until he grinned at her.

She gave him a glass of sherry and excused herself to toss the salad and open the wine. Dave followed her to the kitchen.

"How long have you lived here?" he asked curiously.

"A few months. My aunt and uncle are traveling."

"Where did you live before that?"

"Here and there. Connecticut, mostly."

"You're being mysterious," Dave muttered in her ear. "You don't want to admit your shady past."

"No, I don't," she agreed with an edge of sadness.

His arm came around her waist, and his fingers stroked across her belly. The other hand lightly clasped her breast. "You feel like real silk."

Rowen took a deep breath, wanting to turn in his arms and forget the gourmet meal, but she made herself remember that he was there for a reason. They had some talking to do.

"As long as you're hanging around"—she handed him the salad—"put this on the table."

Dave carried it out and was back in seconds. She unwrapped the bottle of wine he had brought and thanked him. It was red. She explained that they were having seafood and that she had already chilled some white wine."

"Save it for another time," Dave said easily. "I like your sexy outfit. I'd like nothing better than to strip it off you."

She frowned. "Not so fast."

"I know." He sighed. "We have to talk."

"You had plenty to say the other morning," she reminded him.

"And now I have to unsay it. I mean, I *want* to!" he stressed.

The casserole contained scallops, shrimp and crabmeat. She put it on the table, along with feathery rice and new peas. Dave poured the wine, and they sat down. Rowen's eyes narrowed. What if Dave really was what he had claimed—a charming bastard who didn't want to settle for one woman? But now that he knew she had money, he'd decided to play her along. Pearl's excellent meal seemed to stick in her throat.

Clancy wandered into the dining room and stretched out near the fireplace. Vicky lay under the table, panting gently.

"These rugs are beautiful," Dave remarked. "The colors are so bright and rich. . . . Should Clancy be shedding on them? I could put him in the kitchen."

"Oh, no. He looks so comfortable. What did you mean, he's been nervous? He seems perfectly relaxed now."

"This afternoon he was pacing the floor and howling. I had to take him outside three times. My next-door neighbor insisted on giving him tuna this morning. It might have been spoiled."

"Did you take him to the vet?"

"Because he was throwing up?" Dave looked at her curiously. "Dogs throw up all the time. Sorry, this is hardly a conversation for the dinner table."

They laughed, then talked about what they'd been doing since they last saw each other, tiptoeing around mention of the way they had parted.

Dave praised the food. "This is delicious."

"Thank you. I'll tell Pearl." Rowen took a swallow of wine. "I can cook, too, you know. I took several courses at cooking school." It wasn't her fault she hadn't put them into practice. Joe had preferred dining out expensively—to see and be seen.

For dessert she had bought mouth-watering *babas au rum* at an excellent French pastry shop on First Avenue. Dave ate every last crumb and sat back with a sigh.

"Rowen, that was a dinner to be remembered!" He laid his napkin on the table and picked up his coffee cup, then followed her back into the spacious sitting room. They sat on one of the elegantly upholstered couches arranged in front of the fireplace.

A grand piano dominated the area in front of the big front window. Another seating area was nearby. Scattered about the rest of the room was the kind of furniture Dave had seen only in the windows of the fancier antique shops: ornate Oriental tables; carved black urns spouting feathery dried fronds; oil paintings in valuable frames. Everything gleamed from careful polishing, but Dave found the room dismaying.

Rowen might look like a waif elsewhere, but she fit the richness of these surroundings. Her shiny seal-brown hair and white skin, and the dark, vibrant colors she chose to wear, made her seem like a woman from another century, or from his imagination. Dave studied her with fascination. Her eyes shone like jewels. Pearl earrings on her delicate earlobes glowed, then disappeared behind the shining fall of her hair as she turned her head. In this setting she made him think of a painting by some seventeenth-century master.

How could he ever have thought of letting her go?

She had bewitched him. He had been so sure of what he wanted—what he would and would not do. Then she had tumbled into his life with her absurd dog. Since the other morning he had been considering not a full-time job, but maybe a part-time one. Two days a week. Or three. He studied her. To look at her was to reach for her. . . .

Rowen slipped out of his arms on the pretext of carrying their empty coffee cups to the kitchen. Returning, she took crystal snifters from the Art Deco bar near the middle of the room and splashed brandy into them. At last she came to sit sideways on the couch, one knee drawn up so she could talk to him.

"Dave . . ."

"I suppose you're used to this kind of living," he said thoughtfully.

"What kind of living?"

"This!" He waved his hand at the room. "Silk outfits, rosebuds on the table, French pastries."

"I . . . the pastries weren't expensive, if that's what you mean."

"That's *not* what I mean! I mean being surrounded by expensive comfort."

She shrugged. "I hadn't thought about it one way or the other."

Dave was silent while he sloshed the well-aged liquor around in the bottom of his glass. At last he looked up at her, his well-formed mouth crooked in a lopsided smile.

"You mean a lot to me, Rowen. Ever since Vicky latched onto me, you've been on my mind. I felt like such a failure—saying I couldn't afford you—but after the wild and wonderful way we made love, I felt really trapped. I knew if I put my cartoons aside and got a full-time job, I'd turn into such a grouch you'd end up hating me. And I'd be feeling like a martyr. What we had—have

—is too rare to go to pieces that way. It seemed better . . . I thought I was doing the right thing by ending it abruptly. I didn't want you to think I was rejecting you because you didn't have much money. I decided you'd be hurt less if you thought I was a class-A heel."

"Why did you think I was poor?" Rowen studied him with interest. "Because I'm underweight?"

"I wanted to think you needed me, I guess." Unable to keep from touching her, Dave squeezed her knee. "My God, the barriers we put up for ourselves! At the same time that I thought you needed me, I was telling myself I couldn't let you into my life."

Rowen studied him indulgently. She reached for his hand and laughed. "You don't turn off your creative imagination when you quit work, do you?"

Dave smiled with relief. "When you told me you had enough money to live on, I saw I'd been kidding myself. I guess I'd been trying to resist my gut feelings. They were telling me, 'Here's the love of your life, Archer,' and I was running like a chicken, screaming I couldn't afford it. After you leveled with me, I had to come to terms with reality. Can you forgive me?"

Rowen held nothing back from her smile of assent. Before she could throw herself into his arms, she heard the front door open.

"Rowen!" Celia's voice caroled.

Damn! Celia! "A friend of mine stays here, too," Rowen explained hastily.

"I had a fight with Roberto." Celia entered the room with vivacity. Clearly the fight hadn't depressed her. At the sight of Dave she checked herself. "Oh, I'm sorry! I didn't mean to intrude. I forgot you were having company."

Dave came to his feet, and Rowen introduced him. Celia looked him up and down with admiration.

"So you're the man Vicky bit!" she said mischievously. "She *does* have good taste. I said so when Rowen described you."

Dave laughed. Obviously he was used to women coming on

strong. Celia certainly looked attractive, and Dave clearly appreciated every curve. Rowen fought against a shiver of jealousy.

"Will you have some brandy with us?" she invited.

"No, no." Celia declined. "I'm going upstairs. I am going to do one thing, though, now that I've met your handsome friend." She flicked him an audacious smile. "I'm going to invite him to our cocktail party Friday night, unless you've already done so. Has she invited you?" she demanded of Dave.

"No," he said, cocking his head at Rowen.

"Why are you keeping this charming man hidden?" Celia asked with a disarming smile, and then bit her lip. Rowen guessed she was remembering Rowen's careless remark of weeks ago: "If I ever bring him home, don't forget I'm the house sitter."

"He's shy," Rowen said teasingly, and Dave grinned.

"Dave, I work on the principle that a party can never have too many single men." Celia smiled archly. "Do invite him, Rowen." She held out her hand. Dave shook it, looking bemused.

"Look, I do want you to come," Rowen began. "I hadn't gotten around to mentioning it."

Dave wasn't listening. He exclaimed, "Oh-oh!" and made a dash for the dining room.

Rowen had no trouble recognizing the sound that had alerted him. It was the unmistakable gagging of an animal about to throw up.

"Clancy! Not on the rug!" he shouted.

While Rowen stood helplessly wondering what to do, Dave appeared with Clancy in his arms and strode toward the entrance.

"Open the door, quick!" he called over his shoulder.

Rowen complied. Clancy was promptly and distressingly sick on the outside step.

Dave looked apologetic. "Better than on the rug."

"Sure, it's no problem. But what are you going to do about him now?" Rowen worried.

"Take him home and give him some medicine I have." Dave bent to stroke his dog. "Poor old fellow!" He straightened up, looking rueful. "I'm sorry. First, I'll clean up this mess."

"Don't worry about it."

"I insist!"

"I don't even know where the cleaning things are kept," she protested. "It's raining again. The rain will wash it away."

Dave raised an eyebrow. "Not used to cleaning, are you? Put your coat on and keep an eye on this mutt. I'll find what I need."

She let him take charge. The dog was his, after all. With the aid of newspapers, a sponge and a bucket of water, Dave briskly washed the steps. He returned the implements to the kitchen and came back wearing his coat.

"Sorry to eat and run." He cupped her cheek with his warm hand. "But I'd better get him home where he can throw up in peace."

Rowen thought of Dave's bare floors and cozy bedroom and smiled wistfully. "Of course, but if he isn't better by tomorrow—"

"—I'll take him to the vet. And no more leftovers from the old lady!" Dave had directed his last comment to Clancy. He drew Rowen into his arms. The current between them flowed again, fierce and exciting.

"Did we finish our discussion?"

"I guess so," Rowen murmured. He had explained pretty straightforwardly what had gone on in his mind. If it was true. . . .

"I'll see you Friday evening, then. I'll talk to you before then. You can call me, too, you know. In fact, it would be nice."

"I'm glad you can come Friday," Rowen told him, ready to linger on the steps as long as he would. "The party is Celia's idea. I wasn't looking forward to it much."

"You bet I'm coming! With all those single men she's rounding up, I want to keep an eye on you . . . ." He tapped her chin with his gloved fist, dropped a final heart-stopping kiss on her lips and led Clancy away.

Dazed and happy, Rowen stepped into the warm hallway. Seeing Dave, spending time with him, had dissolved her fears for the time being. Surely he was being honest with her; surely he had come tonight because he wanted to see her, not because he wanted to see how well off she was. He hadn't looked around the house with an assessing air. He hadn't inquired where her uncle got his money, or where she got hers, or been particularly impressed by the furnishings.

Of course, he could be biding his time. . . .

She took Vicky out for her final walk of the day and tried to think sensibly, but her emotions were chaotic. One minute she was happy Dave had returned; the next she felt sure he had an ulterior motive.

She hated herself for thinking that way, but the past had taught her a hard lesson. You were supposed to learn by experience. That sounded good. In practice, experience was different each time. Try as she would, she couldn't compare Dave to Joe. If Dave was an opportunist, he was a mighty clever one.

Upstairs she undressed and slipped between the satin sheets. Her aunt definitely went in for elegance. She smiled to herself. Despite the elegance of her aunt's home, all Dave's attention had been for her.

When she thought about the party, she was annoyed at Celia. She had been reluctant to expose Dave to the arrogant professional men Celia knew: doctors, lawyers, securities analysts. Dave would feel out of place. They would be coming from their offices and wearing suits.

Finally she decided not to worry about minor details. Dave would be fine. He was sophisticated enough to know what to wear.

Dave arrived at the party in an expectant mood. He was looking forward to seeing Rowen again against her own background, where she didn't look like a waif at all. It was better to see her that way: realistically.

By the time he'd been in the house a quarter of an hour, he

remembered that he hated cocktail parties. This one should have been different, because of Rowen, but he hadn't had a chance to say a word to her in private.

He had looked forward to talking to her while he enjoyed his drink, watching and commenting on the other guests. Instead, she was greeting people and rushing around. The crowd was young, chic, upper crust. Men outnumbered women two to one. Celia had meant what she said.

Still, he rather enjoyed the novelty of being able to stand in a corner with his drink and not be accosted by a succession of females. Thoughtfully he watched Rowen perform as hostess.

He got a kick out of watching her. She had such poise, and she seemed quite at home in these fancy surroundings. Her grandparents must have been well-to-do. Old Lyme was one of those posh towns. It occurred to him to wonder how big a trust fund she had. Was she house-sitting to help out her aunt or herself?

She was wearing a dark dress of some filmy material that swirled around her knees, and high-heeled sandals. She had pretty legs as well as a pretty face. Tonight she didn't look thin, only delicate.

Where was Vicky this evening, he wondered. Banished to the nether regions for fear she would take a death grip on someone? She wouldn't do that, he thought, and then laughed at himself. He wanted his experience with Rowen and Vicky to be unique.

Rowen was laughing now with two men in dark suits, lawyers or accountants by the looks of their vests and cuffed trousers. One put his arm around her, and Dave stiffened. The other didn't appear to like it much, either. He was doing his best to hold Rowen's attention by dominating the conversation.

"Dave!" He heard his name spoken and turned to see Celia regarding him, her eyes perfectly made up, her red lips smiling.

"Why are you standing in the corner?"

"Wasn't that why I was invited—to make the room look full?" he asked with gentle irony.

"Certainly!" She laughed back at him. "But you're allowed

to talk to the other guests. Stewart—" She intercepted a passing male. "This is Dave Archer."

The man paused and shook Dave's hand. "Stewart Sawyer." Blond hair was swept smoothly back from his forehead. His suit and shirt and fingernails were immaculate. Inside his charcoal-gray suit he carried himself like an athlete.

"Dave's a cartoonist," Celia said. "Talk to him." She flitted away.

Stewart shook his head and grinned with understanding. "How's your drink?" he asked, peering into Dave's glass. "Nearly empty! Let me get you a refill. What are you drinking?"

"Bourbon and water."

Stewart took Dave's glass. "Back in a jiff."

The man's air of consequence, or perhaps his Ivy League accent, made the hair on the back of Dave's neck rise. He didn't like the fellow's tie, either. Old-school stripes. Yet he seemed friendly. Dave knew he was being guilty of pure prejudice. Or did he sense competition? Were all these single men interested in Celia, or did a discerning few save their attentions for Rowen?

Stewart returned with their refilled glasses and ranged himself alongside Dave, making easy conversation. Dave recognized that his dislike stemmed, in part, from the fact that Stewart was at ease in this room. Dave knew himself to be an outsider. He wouldn't have cared, except that this was Rowen's scene. How would she feel about fitting into his life?

"So you're a cartoonist," Stewart said.

Dave started. He had momentarily forgotten his companion.

"Where'd you meet Celia?" Stewart inquired. Dave took a dislike to the amused tone of his question. It intimated that Celia had been slumming.

"Here at the house. I'm a friend of Rowen's."

His explanation appeared to alert the other man. "Where'd you meet Rowen?" he demanded.

"On the street. Her dog took a fancy to my pants leg. We struck up quite an acquaintance before Vicky decided to let go."

"I knew that dog would get her into trouble." Stewart clearly classed Dave as "trouble."

Dave decided it was his turn to ask a question. "Where did you meet Celia?"

"I've known Celia and Rowen both since they were in braces. I went to school with Celia's brothers."

Dave conceded that the other man had a very valid claim to be present. He decided to let the man know he wasn't interested in insinuating himself into Celia's life.

"Rowen seems to know most of these people," he commented, and received a strange look. "I mean, I gathered it was Celia's party. I understand Rowen's only been in town a few months, and she strikes me as a bit of a loner."

Stewart looked him up and down. "You can't expect a clear field."

His hard look made Dave bristle, but he held his tongue and his temper. What was the guy telling him?

"Word gets around fast—unfortunately," Stewart went on. "But Rowen is particular. Usually." He gave Dave another appraising look. His meaning was clear. "Been seeing a lot of her?"

Dave's eyes narrowed. He knew how to deal with nosy bastards, no matter at what level of society. He drew himself up, pleased to see he was two inches taller than the other man. "I can't see as that's any of your business," he drawled, his southern Missouri accent marked.

Stewart returned his glare. "Don't think you'll have easy sailing," he said arrogantly. "There are others in the race."

"What the hell do you mean?" Dave growled, his anger rising.

Before Stewart could answer, Rowen popped up in front of them. "Oh! You two have met!"

"We have," Dave said, as pleasantly as he could manage.

She touched the other man's sleeve. "Stewart, would you be a pal? I've only had one martini this whole time. Every time I go to get another one, somebody pulls me into a conversation, or the doorbell rings. . . ."

"Of course!" Stewart disappeared as though glad of an excuse. Dave's hackles settled back down when he felt Rowen's hand slip into his.

"Sorry I've been so busy," she apologized. "Have you met anyone besides Stewart?"

"A few." He shrugged. "They're not exactly my type. . . ."

"I was afraid they wouldn't be." Rowen smiled at him, and his heart turned over.

"Let's get out of here," he muttered. "Let's go someplace quiet and eat. Let Celia run her own party."

"I can't leave now! Wait till this is over. A bunch of us will probably go out and eat. Let me treat you."

Before Dave could answer, Stewart reappeared with Rowen's cocktail. She let go of Dave's hand to take the glass.

"Rowen, I want to talk to you before I go," Stewart told her. He gave Dave a glance of dislike and moved off.

With an effort Dave fought down his anger. "I get the idea that fellow's got some control over you," he growled.

Rowen shrugged. "His law firm handled my divorce, and he's my financial manager. I've known him forever."

"So he said." Had Stewart himself handled her divorce? Listened to her confidences? Comforted her when she was hurt? Perhaps because Dave had had more bourbon than usual, the fact that the other man knew more about Rowen's life than he did made him see red. His mind surged with jealousy and possessiveness and all the turbulent emotions he liked to believe never affected him. Anger and frustration suddenly came to the surface.

"You really like this scene, don't you?"

"What do you mean?"

"All this solid money and background! No wonder you look like a waif when you leave here. You're lost out there!"

"You're imagining things again!" she said sharply. Some latecomers arrived, and she went to welcome them.

Dave's stomach constricted with cold fear. He wasn't imagining this set-up. Rowen was out of his reach. His earnings, even teamed with a small trust fund, could never add up to this opulence.

So what? There were more important things in life than fancy furniture. Running with this crowd hadn't gotten her a decent husband, judging from what she'd said. Still, he should have guessed that things wouldn't be as easy as just solving the financial problem.

She needed someone to care for *her,* not to keep up appearances. Dave looked around, his jaw thrust forward. He didn't see a man here who looked good enough for Rowen. And she certainly didn't need fancy furniture to make her happy. But did she know that?

Dave saw no point in hanging around in order to go to an expensive restaurant with a party of people and maybe not have Rowen to himself the whole evening. The idea that she thought she had to offer to pay his way was galling. He could afford expensive restaurants—once a month, maybe. But if he spent that kind of money, he wanted Rowen's exclusive attention.

He crossed the room to her. "No thanks on the dinner invitation," he said. "I'll call you soon."

"Are you leaving?" Her eyes were imploring, but he hardened his heart. She mustn't think she could fit him into this high-flying crowd. No way! There would have to be compromises.

How much money did she have, anyway? Not that it mattered; he was determined to have her. Judging from the people around her tonight, she still needed his protection.

He gave her a good-bye wave, retrieved his trench coat and left the house, feeling gloomy. He had to have her, no matter what the obstacles.

7

Saturday the bookstore was busy. The late-March sunshine seemed to bring out all the browsers in New York, but in between helping customers Rowen still found time to brood. She didn't know whether she was glad or sorry that Dave had left the party so abruptly.

After he'd gone, the gathering had fallen decidedly flat. Her heart hadn't been in any danger of being touched by either of the two men who had vied so flatteringly for her attention at the club where the group wound up. She wished she could have left with Dave, as he had suggested, but it would have been too impolite to her other guests.

What did she want? A safe life with the kind of people she knew? Her friends were busy enjoying themselves, off in France, Switzerland, Bermuda, Colorado. She had turned her back on that when she joined Horace in the bookshop. On the other hand, could she face the turmoil and adjustments she would have to make if this obsession with Dave continued? The answer was complicated. She didn't want the turmoil, but she wanted Dave.

Each time the telephone rang, she caught her breath. Each time the call was about books.

Then Stewart Sawyer phoned and invited her to dinner to talk business. She hesitated before accepting, but it didn't look like Dave was going to call. The talk with Stewart was something she couldn't put off forever.

That evening, Stewart took her to a new restaurant that she and Dave had passed while walking the dogs. Dave had once mentioned that they would try it when it opened. Now here she was.

For an instant she felt disloyal, but it was impossible to go elsewhere. She had already admitted that she'd never been there. She caught herself surveying the other diners, half expecting to meet Dave's accusing eyes.

Stewart did his best to capture her attention. "This is a celebration!" he announced. "I didn't want to tell you last night—I wanted to make it a special occasion. Remember that stock we bought for you last month—good, solid blue-chip stuff guaranteed not to move more than a point in either direction? Right after we bought it, it began to move, and it's still climbing! Old Smith wanted to sell this week—after all, he's the senior partner—but we convinced him to hang in. If I can keep him from losing his nerve, in a few months you'll be back where you were before you married." He looked proud of himself.

Rowen smiled approval, though the subject bored her so much that she didn't even ask the stock's name.

"I hope you bought some for yourself," she commented.

Dave couldn't possibly be in the restaurant, but she scanned the other diners anyway. She tended to see him in every big, brown-haired man in the room.

"You don't look very happy about it," Stewart prodded. "I thought you'd be pleased. You can forget you ever had a drain on your resources."

"You think that's all there is to forgetting a bad marriage?"

Stewart watched the waiter pop the cork on the champagne he'd ordered before answering. Rowen watched Stewart. He was the picture of the young, upwardly mobile East Sider—the clothes, the haircut, the manner. If the men in the restaurant suddenly played musical chairs, their dates would hardly notice the change.

After the waiter had filled their glasses, Stewart raised his. "That kind of a win on the stock exchange should make everything rosy."

"I'll use some of it to buy a condo," Rowen said. "My aunt called. She and my uncle are coming home sometime next week."

"You'll be able to afford anything you want." He raised his glass again. "Here's to you, kid."

She raised her glass. The dinner would probably be charged against the administrative expenses of her trust, so she might as well enjoy it. Would Dave—if he knew—be excited by Stewart's news? She wished there were some way to find out.

She drank two glasses of champagne, hoping it would dissolve her stomach's resistance to the idea of food. Doggedly she worked her way through her *scampi*, half listening to Stewart's comments on Celia's party.

Suddenly he said, "Your so-called cartoonist didn't seem too comfortable at the party."

Rowen's fork paused in midair. Her eyes flew to his face. "What do you mean?"

Stewart's supercilious smile reminded her why she didn't like him. She was wasting her breath to ask. He wouldn't tell her. He was after her reaction.

"I asked for his credentials, speaking as your trustee."

"You didn't!"

"Oh, not right out," he said blandly. "I understand you met over Vicky. What makes you think he's really a cartoonist?"

"I've seen his cartoons!"

Stewart dropped the subject then and put himself out to be amusing. Rowen told herself that other men besides Dave could make her laugh. But other men didn't give her what felt like a blow to the heart when she met them on the street.

She and Stewart left the restaurant and were walking back to her house when Stewart took her arm. She was laughing at something he'd said and didn't see Dave until he was only a few steps away. Their eyes met and locked. Dave's blazed like a jet of blue gas—cool colored, but burning.

She didn't know afterward whether she nodded to him or not. It hardly mattered. Their eyes had met and exchanged signals that stirred her to the depths. By an act of will she had kept from turning to look after him.

"Wasn't that your cartoonist?"

"Yes," she choked. What would Dave do now? Did the fury in his eyes mean he would never call again?

Almost in silence she let Stewart take her home and kiss her good-night. On the step he took her by the arms and shook her playfully.

"What's with you?"

"Stewart, I'm sorry. I'm a little tired. Thank you for dinner. I'm really proud of you for making a killing with such a stodgy stock."

"I get the feeling you find me about as interesting as that stock." He gave her a bitter smile and strode off.

She forgot Stewart as soon as she shut the door. What would Dave be thinking? He hadn't asked for a commitment. He'd gone casually off, saying he'd call. Was she supposed to stay home and wait? Would he believe that she and Stewart had been having a business dinner? When she recalled the way his eyes had shot blue sparks, she knew he wouldn't.

Monday morning Dave sat at his drawing board and thought about Rowen. He hadn't stopped thinking about her since meeting her arm in arm with another man. Where had he expected her to be on Saturday night, at home with her dog?

He had meant to call her as soon as the bookshop opened Saturday morning, but he'd started working, and the hours had slipped away. For once he cursed his ability to concentrate.

103

Why hadn't she called *him?* When he finally *had* called, the line had been busy. The next time he thought about it, the bookstore was closed. He could have tried telephoning her at home, but he had been afraid that by that time she would have had other plans. As she *had!*

Anger rose in him like a black tide. He had thought everything was patched up between them. And there she was, prancing around with someone else.

He hadn't really seen the man. His accusing eyes had met Rowen's and been trapped in their depths. He was pretty sure her escort had been that irritating guy who had said there were others in the race. What race, for Pete's sake?

He knew he had a talent for looking beneath the surface and seeing amusing and endearing qualities in people and animals —qualities most observers overlooked. That was what made his cartoons poignant. Rowen was sweet, and certainly pretty, but he didn't see why suitors should be lining up for her. Unless she had more money than she had let on.

Uneasily he wondered if other men wanted to protect her, too. He dropped his pen on the taboret beside his drawing table and stalked to the kitchen, where he spooned instant coffee into a cup. The trouble with drawing was that you had time to think.

Waiting for the kettle to boil, he went on thinking about Rowen. He couldn't help feeling concerned for her.

Stewart had struck Dave as domineering. Rowen didn't need someone pushing her around. Dave had assumed she wasn't dating other men. She always looked so wistful that he couldn't help feeling she was alone and needed him.

Of course, she always denied that she needed to be protected. She was quick to pull out her billfold for taxis, and she bought expensive wine.

But was she eating enough?

Back at work, he couldn't escape the feeling that she needed him. He wanted to take her under his wing and look after her, whether she liked it or not.

He felt about her as he did about Clancy and Harrison the cat, who, he had discovered, was now clearly Ms. Harrison. She had escaped via the fire escape and enjoyed two heady spring nights of courtship on the roof. Doubtless she was counting on Dave to support her offspring.

He went back to thinking about Rowen. How much money did she have? Surely not a lot or she wouldn't be working, would she? Really rich people didn't work. They sat on museum committees.

He laid aside the finished drawing and stretched. Maybe he had made her mad by walking out of the party. He should have called on Saturday morning, before he began to concentrate on his project.

In the kitchen he opened a can of tuna fish, then took two bites of the sandwich he made. He laid it down and dialed Rowen's shop. He didn't care how deep a canyon lay between her life-style and his. There had to be a way to get her to cross it. From what he'd seen on Sutton Place, he could give her more of the important things in life than anyone else was giving her. Love, happiness, warmth, humor.

Love? Had he really said love? His heart thumped. He put the phone back on the hook and stared into space, his smile bemused. Then he picked up the phone and dialed her number again.

It seemed to ring endlessly, but at last she picked it up.

"Rowen, it's Dave." His voice went tight with anxiety. What if she'd decided that she preferred her elegantly vacuous friends and surroundings? He remembered how she had been arm in arm with that creep.

"Yes?" She sounded so aloof!

"If you're free tonight," he drawled cautiously, "I'd like to take you to dinner."

"Oh, Dave, I'd love to go!"

He closed his eyes with relief. She hadn't crossed him off. He arranged to meet her at the bookshop. They would take Vicky home, and she would give Dave a drink while she changed.

When he hung up he felt as thrilled as if he'd just made his first date.

Rowen put the phone back on its cradle in a state of exhilaration. Four hours from now she'd be with him. She slipped back to the storeroom and looked in the mirror. "You were going to be cautious this time around," she reminded herself.

"But Dave's so different. He has integrity and character and honor—all the old-fashioned virtues."

"How can you be sure?"

Rowen looked thoughtfully at her image. She would have to tell Dave that she was looking for an apartment. What if he asked her to move in with him? She couldn't! It was too big a step. Besides, there wasn't room.

More likely he'd want to move in with *her*. He'd suggest she buy a big condo—or a loft. And then she'd know . . . what? That he was taking advantage of her? A bigger place made sense if two people were thinking of living together. She drew a deep breath, then exhaled. She could only wait and see how he behaved.

She left the bookshop a few minutes early. Horace would lock up. She could see Dave waiting on the curb, out of the stream of homeward-bound pedestrians. She had never seen him so well dressed, he had dressed for her in a supple suede jacket over a shirt. And a necktie! His well-pressed trousers were a deeper tan than his jacket. He had an artist's eye for combining colors.

"How nice you look!" she exclaimed before becoming lost in his caressing gaze. "Are we going someplace special?"

"Anywhere with you is special." He tucked her free hand under his arm. "Let's get out of this crowd."

On the side street they could walk without worrying that someone would fall over Vicky. Dave stopped and turned her to face him.

"Honey, I'm sorry I didn't call sooner. I started working

Saturday, and the time just disappeared. That's something you have to understand about me. That's the way I work. Yesterday I had to finish the job so I could deliver it. Now, tell me why you went out with that guy Stewart."

He wasn't scowling, but his face had taken on a dark look. That or the chill wind made Rowen shiver.

"It was a business dinner," she stated. "Strictly business."

"On Saturday night?"

She shrugged. "It was as good a time as any." She shook herself free and continued walking. "Is this why you asked me out? To . . . to grill me?"

"I want to find out where I stand," he growled, pacing alongside.

"Where do you want to stand?"

"It's not a question of 'want!' You know what's between us as well as I do! I have the sense of having found the other part of myself. You *must* feel it! Whatever struck me struck you, too. For better or worse. Rowen . . ." He stopped again and cupped her face in his hands. People on the way home passed them on the left and right, as though they were two boulders in a stream. "Am I right?"

Her brown eyes met his questioning blue ones before she lowered long lashes. "Perhaps."

"You know it!" Dave dropped a light kiss on her lips. Taking her arm again, he swung her into his stride. He began humming something so off-key that Rowen couldn't recognize it.

"You've got a favorable audience," she laughed. "People are smiling at us."

"Good! We make them remember what it's like to be in love. I feel like a kid out with his first date. Out to enjoy himself. He doesn't know the pitfalls."

Love! "Must there be pitfalls?"

"Life is one enormous pitfall. Don't talk me out of that! That outlook is what makes my cartoons funny."

"I wouldn't dream of it, then." Rowen let her spirits soar with his. She began to have the feeling that she was dancing.

At the house she meant to give him a drink while she fed Vicky and changed, but as soon as she led him into the elegant sitting room he caught her in his arms.

"Oh, Rowen, my love!" He kissed her hungrily, then held her away so he could feast his eyes on her face. "I do love you, you know. Do you love me?"

She gazed at him, her heart in her eyes. "Yes, Dave." When had it happened? Days ago, perhaps. She had been too fearful to think about it until now.

He squeezed her so tightly that she squealed in protest. His kiss was hard and claiming and exuberant. "There may be pitfalls ahead, but we'll get around them. We'll be philosophical, like my cartoon people."

"As long as we don't look like them!" Rowen giggled.

"What's wrong with their looks?"

"Oh, you know! They look like losers."

"They've fallen victim to a lot of those pitfalls I was talking about, but they're trying to enjoy themselves until the next catastrophe."

"That's so sad!"

"It's laughing at the guy who slips on a banana peel because it could have been you."

Rowen shivered. How delicately poised they were on the brink of disaster! Or loneliness. What if Vicky hadn't tackled Dave that night on the street?

Dave caught her to him. "Don't worry about it! They're only jokes. I bet you wouldn't find a pitfall between here and Missouri."

He pulled her down onto the couch and began kissing her in earnest.

"Vicky's starving," she protested. "And Celia could come in anytime."

Dave widened his eyes in mock horror and smoothed his hair. "I don't want to fall into Celia's net again."

"Didn't you like my friends?" she asked lightly.

"Not a damn one!" he said, his tone suddenly serious. "I had the feeling the men were all after something. What?"

Rowen avoided his eye. "You're imagining things again." She bestowed a kiss on the bridge of his nose and took her eagerly prancing dog to the kitchen. In her bedroom she changed into one of the designer creations she owned but seldom wore. It was rich, deep amber and positively dripped with sheer material. Over it she wore a light cashmere coat.

Dave took her to the restaurant where she had gone with Stewart. Fate was conspiring to rewrite the scene the way she wanted it. Tonight everything was perfect. She felt as close to Dave as if she'd known him forever. Forever stretched into the future, too.

When their dinner arrived, she took a deep breath. What would he say to her decision to move into a place of her own—a place where she could be free to share more of his life.

"My aunt and uncle are coming back sometime this month. Celia's moving to Boston, and I'm going to take an apartment."

Dave stopped chewing. His face had an arrested look. "When?" he demanded around a bite of steak.

Lovingly, she admired the strong line of his jaw. "In a couple of weeks."

He leaned toward her across the table, his eyes intent. "Move in with me."

She was silent, wondering if she had the nerve to do something so crazy. No! Living with him would be too much like being married, even though she'd spend her money and he'd spend his. It might be safe from that angle, but there were too many other dangers. She shrank back in her chair. His place was impossibly Spartan, for one thing. She couldn't imagine herself living so frugally.

"It's out of the question," she said sharply.

"Why?"

She threw up her hands and said the first thing that came to mind. "Where would I keep my clothes?"

"Your clothes! Is that the only objection you can think of?"

"You don't know how many I have!"

"What difference does it make?" he asked impatiently. "You probably have far too many, and you don't wear most of them.

Honey, if we're going to share our lives, we're both going to have to make some changes."

She avoided his eyes in order to hide the fear in her own. "It's too soon! We barely know each other."

Dave reached for her hand. "I've known you since we crawled out of the slime together a million years ago."

"Then there's no hurry, is there? I'll find a place somewhere in this area."

"Think about it," he urged. The idea of having her in his bed every night made any sacrifice worthwhile. "I could get some decent furniture. I don't need a whole bare room for a studio. . . ."

"Yes, you do. I wouldn't dream of upsetting your arrangements."

"You can upset any arrangement I have!"

"Very gallant! But I'm used to more room." She hesitated, testing him. "Maybe we could find a bigger place we could share. . . ."

"If you mean a loft, forget it! They cost the earth. I couldn't afford *half* the rent. I don't think you could, either." He waited, wondering if she would name a sum she could afford. Instead she looked vague and shrugged. Dave reached across the table, unable to resist touching her cheek. He smiled into her eyes. "What would I have done if you didn't like dogs?"

Her smile glinted in return. "How would we have met if I didn't like dogs?"

"We would have met somehow."

"Fate?"

Rowen's mysterious smile heated his blood. "I wonder about this strange behavior called courtship," he said impatiently. "Here we are dining in a restaurant when all I'm thinking about is taking you home to bed. Yet even birds have courtship rites. They go through all sorts of weird gyrations before getting down to basics."

"Perhaps it's nature's way of building tension."

"I'm not criticizing! It just seems curious. And wonderful. Every moment with you is wonderful."

After dinner they strolled to Dave's building. Rowen delighted in walking down the street on his arm. They climbed the stairs as though the rest of the evening had been prearranged. It had been, Rowen thought. It was programmed in their genes, in their intense longing for each other.

Dave unlocked his door, switched on the light and took her in his arms.

"Every night I dream of having you like this," he murmured, his lips against her hair. He took her coat from her. "Did I tell you that's a beautiful dress?" he asked. "It's perfect on you—you're perfect in it."

Something furry rubbed against Rowen's ankles. She looked down to see Dave's cat. Making a strange sound that was half purr, half meow, it moved on to rub against Dave's legs.

"Is that Harrison?" she exclaimed. "He's gotten—oh-oh."

"Exactly," Dave said. *"She's* going to present me with kittens any day."

The cat rubbed against his legs and meowed louder.

"What's wrong with you?" Dave asked the animal as he carried their coats into the bedroom. The cat followed them, wailing pitifully.

"You don't suppose . . . ?" Shocked, he turned to stare at Rowen.

"Don't ask *me!*"

"I made her a bed in the closet. Maybe that's what she wants. The door's shut."

He opened it. The cat continued to twine about his legs. He reached for hangers, saying as he did so, "Better hang these up, unless we want—Harrison! For Pete's sake, will you go tend to your business?"

"She's frightened," Rowen said, picking the cat up and sitting on the bed with her. "Are these her first kittens?"

"First and last! If I hadn't thought she was a tomcat, I'd have had her spayed."

"Your innocence is touching."

"Oh, is it!" Dave pulled her down to lie beside him. Disturbed by the commotion, Harrison jumped to the floor and left the room.

"That's it!" Dave commended. "Give us some privacy."

Rowen stretched her impatient body against Dave's. Desire warmed her limbs. Dave's mouth found hers, and she sank into bliss. All feeling and all thought were dedicated to enjoying the exquisite pressure of his lips, the thrust of his tongue, the solidity of his body against hers. Her eyes closed, she was dimly aware of sounds—Dave's excited breathing and her own, the wail of a siren on the avenue. They were meant to be together. Nothing could keep them apart. She returned his kisses, and time slipped away.

Dave raised his head and leaned over her. "Honey, shouldn't you take off this beautiful dress?" He slid the tiny straps off her shoulders and touched his lips to the white skin where the dress ended. Before she had time to savor the thrill, he raised his head.

"Oh, my God!"

Rowen opened her eyes to see his horrified face turned to something on the quilt beyond her. She turned over, supporting herself on one elbow.

The cat was curled in a hollow of the quilt. A kitten was emerging from beneath her tail.

Rowen caught her breath. Dave pulled her up to sit with her back against his chest. They watched in awe as new life emerged into the world.

"She was waiting for us to come home and keep her company!" Dave's chest vibrated with laughter. Rowen felt a jolt of sharp disappointment. She slid out of his arms and stood up, trying not to gag at the sight before her.

"I'd like some wine! Do you have any?" Without looking at the bed again she made for the kitchen and opened the refrigerator. She remembered to brace herself for another encounter with the mannequin's hand, but it no longer hung there.

She found the wine and took out two glasses. Over her shoulder, she saw Dave in the doorway.

"Are you having some?" she asked.

"Sure," Dave grinned. "Let's celebrate the birth of the little beggars."

Rowen took a long swallow and heaved a relieved breath. "I love cats, but I'd just as soon miss this. . . ."

Dave laughed and flung an arm around her. "It's easy to see you didn't grow up on a farm."

"I suppose it is." She gave him a wry smile. "What are you going to do with them?"

"Draw them!"

She should have guessed. "All of them?"

"However many. I hope she doesn't have more than three. It's her first litter. I don't use nearly enough cats in my pictures. Can't you just see my wacky backgrounds with kittens scrambling everywhere?"

She was taken aback by his enthusiasm. If she'd had a whisper of a thought of moving in with him, it was now stilled. With kittens there would be a whole menagerie. Dave hadn't yet seen her Himalayan cats—two darling puffballs, so shy they slipped upstairs like shadows the minute the front door opened.

Pets aside, she had thought that Dave would feel as she did: Tonight the cat was a blasted nuisance. Rowen carried her wineglass into the studio and sat on the lumpy couch. Dave followed. Since the bed was denied them, maybe he would make love to her here.

Before she could twine her arms around his neck, he said, "I better see how she's making out."

Clancy was taking no interest in anything but getting his rest. Rowen called to him. He raised his head to look at her, thumped his tail and closed his eyes again. Rowen sipped her wine and brooded about being upstaged by a cat.

Dave came out of the bedroom after a few minutes and closed the door.

"The count is up to two. She's doing all right by herself."

"Good." Rowen opened her arms to him, but the fire had gone out of their embrace.

"Where are you going to sleep?" she asked. "Want to come to my place? Celia will be asleep by now."

Dave ran his fingers through her silky hair with its golden highlights and kissed the tip of her nose.

"Honey, I can't go off and leave the poor thing."

"I didn't think you were that sentimental!" Rowen felt almost sick with disappointment. "Cats have been having kittens by themselves for millions of years."

"Women can have babies alone, too, but that doesn't mean they want to."

"All right! Can you leave her long enough to put me in a taxi?"

"Now you're being sarcastic," he chided.

She wrapped her arms around his chest and laid her face against the fine cotton of his shirt, inhaling his scent. Was she being arrogant? Spoiled? It wasn't Dave's fault his cat had decided to have her kittens on this of all nights.

She looked up at his well-carved mouth. "I guess this is one of those pitfalls you were talking about," she made herself say in an attempt to quiet her hunger for him.

"It sure is!" He grinned regretfully. "I'll get your coat."

Downstairs, he pressed her hands to his lips. "I love you, Rowen. It scares me to think how close I came to shutting you out of my life. I'm sorry about tonight, but I know you understand. . . ."

"I do." She stood on tiptoe to kiss his mouth.

A taxi stopped. Dave opened the door for her.

"I'll call you tomorrow," he promised, and gave the driver her address.

He telephoned the next evening while Rowen was regaling Celia with the story of the kittens.

"Dave here," he said abruptly. "Listen, the people right below me moved out today. My neighbor has the key to the apartment. Want to see it?" He told her what he thought the rent would be. It sounded ridiculously low.

"Uh . . . yes, I guess so. . . ." It hadn't occurred to her that she could rent an apartment in Dave's building. She had been thinking of some new co-ops in the neighborhood.

"Why don't you come over now? Grab a cab—I'll treat you. Bring Vicky and your toothbrush."

Joyful warmth suffused her body. "I'll be right there," she announced, her voice lilting. She hung up and turned to Celia, her face breaking into a smile.

"Your light-o'-love?" Celia raised her eyebrows.

"He wants me to move in below him."

"Good position!" Celia quipped lewdly. "I wouldn't mind having him over me!"

"The apartment below him! He wants me to look at it. Don't wait up! He's treating me to a cab," she added, laughing with light-headed anticipation.

"You're not seriously thinking of moving into the same building?"

"Why not? If things work out, we could get a co-op together later."

"And if they don't work out?"

"Don't say that!"

"Somebody has to! Rowen, you've got stars in your eyes, just like the song says. What happens if you two break up and you have to meet him in the elevator with his new girl friend?"

"The building doesn't have an elevator!" Rowen laughed as though that rendered her friend's warning superfluous.

"No elevator?" Celia raised her hands in supplication. "The stairs, then."

"I could move out," Rowen said, turning serious.

"I know you! You'd be devastated. You wouldn't do anything but sit and quiver."

"Why does everyone assume I'm helpless?"

"Because you are! Oh, not helpless, but vulnerable and sensitive and too proud to stand up for your rights. This is a tough town! There are tough men out there. I wish I hadn't decided to move to Boston."

"What would you do, stick around and look after me?"

"Somebody needs to."

"Then let Dave!" Rowen laughed mischievously and ran upstairs to get her toothbrush.

In the taxi, however, she had second thoughts. What if Celia was right? What if Dave's ardor cooled? There she'd be, stuck in the same building.

Oh, nonsense! If events took that kind of a nose dive, she could leave. Just pack a suitcase and go. Back to her aunt's or to a hotel, never to consider him again. When you weren't married, there were no strings.

"It needs painting, of course," Dave explained as he unlocked the door. "They'll do that when you sign the lease."

Though she liked going to Dave's, she hadn't thought any apartment could look grimmer. This one did. Cockroaches scattered when he turned on the kitchen light. The kitchen window greasily reflected the bare bulb against the outer darkness. The floors were scuffed, the walls grimy. The faucet dripped.

Rowen turned away, revolted, but Dave grabbed her arm. "It's different from Sutton Place, I'll grant you, but it's not expensive as apartments go, and you'd be closer to your shop. Don't look at it the way it is now! Look at the closet space! The bedroom could be as cozy as mine. With fresh paint the place would look altogether different."

The idea of sharing a bigger place with Dave floated into the future, where for safety's sake it belonged. He hadn't even taken up her hint that she could provide larger living quarters. He *wasn't* interested in her money. A load seemed to slip from her shoulders. He wasn't interested in money, and he wasn't interested in capturing her in marriage.

"I'd have carpet put in if I took it," she said consideringly.

"Sure, if you can afford it."

"I could afford it." Rowen looked about her and tried to imagine living in three rooms. Of course, this was Manhattan. Even the new co-ops she'd been thinking of were small. "I don't have to decide tonight, do I?" Her smile wavered.

"Of course not! It would just be so great to have you in the same building."

His appealing look made her heart flutter. Reason flew off into the darkness. What her heart wanted was more compelling. Would he spend his evenings with her? It could be exactly like living together. Should she take a chance?

She drew a deep breath. Against her better judgment she said, "I'll take it."

8

The decision made, Rowen threw herself into getting the apartment ready for her to move into on the first of April. She would make it the kind of place where she and Dave could feel happy and comfortable. They could live close together without any dangerous commitment, though from time to time she was still swept by fear and worry.

Dave wouldn't have the chance to fool her as Joe had, but Dave wasn't that kind of man. He might approach life with a laugh, but he was also honest and sincere. And loving. She rediscovered that daily.

She indulged in an orgy of shopping. As soon as the painters finished—and Rowen was happy to admit that the fresh paint made an enormous difference—she called in an exterminator and a cleaning service. She arranged for a friend of Pearl's to clean weekly. She chose rich gray-blue carpeting for the floors and had new tile with a cheerful red brick pattern laid in the kitchen. She harried the building's managers to send a plumber to fix the worn-out faucets, and considered installing a new sink until Dave talked her out of it.

"Don't spend that kind of money on a place that's not yours! Spend it on stuff you can take when you leave."

Was he already thinking about her leaving? However, she followed his advice. She'd get used to the sink the way it was.

At the end of a week the apartment looked decidedly better, as Dave had promised. Of course, the building was still old. She tried to imagine inviting her aunt and uncle, even Celia, to visit and failed. They would be so shocked! The accommodations weren't like anything she was used to, either, but according to Dave this was an average New York apartment.

She pondered using some of her grandparents' furniture, still stored in Old Lyme, and decided it would be better to buy new pieces scaled to fit the smaller space.

"Buy all new furniture?" Dave cried out in startled protest. She was seated on his couch, leafing through a sale catalog from a smart department store. "You're such an innocent! You'll be in hock for the rest of your life!"

"What else can I do?"

"Buy one piece a month, or something."

"That will take forever. Meantime, my place will be as bare as yours!"

"Where did you live before you came to the city? That's right, you told me you had a house in Connecticut."

"That furniture was sold," she said abruptly as the familiar shame she felt whenever she thought of her marriage swept over her.

"I don't like to think you were married. And unhappy." Dave sank down beside her on the couch and pulled her into his arms. For a time Rowen forgot everything but the delight of their closeness.

"Poor sweetie," Dave said. "I hope he wasn't mean to you."

Rowen pulled away, fire in her eyes. "I am not a poor sweetie! But he was coaxing and sneaky! Pretending to be crazy about me in order to get—" She paused. "In order to get what he wanted."

"I'll remember not to coax you!" Dave squeezed her and made her laugh.

She spent as much as she liked. After all, how extravagant could one get over a three-room apartment? There wasn't room for a dishwasher; there was barely room for the washer-dryer combination. She had never had so much fun, never really enjoyed shopping before, but this was like decorating a honeymoon flat. But safer. Safer and wiser.

To keep the place light and airy she bought wicker. She also kept in mind that Dave was a man, and big. The chairs and couch she chose were solid.

Luckily he was home all day to take the deliveries.

"Aren't you going a little overboard?" he asked, smoothing the fine fabric of the couch. "This must have cost a bundle."

"I want you to be comfortable. And happy."

Dave laughed. "Honey, I could be happy in a shack—with you."

"Well, I couldn't!" She flung herself at him. She wrapped her arms around his chest and pushed her nose into the hollow of his throat, inhaling the wonderful scent of him.

Dave's arms surrounded her. As always, everything but sheer physical attraction went out of their minds.

"Every one of my cells loves every one of your cells," he murmured. "Their ions have a built-in electrical attraction. Scientists haven't discovered it yet, but it's a force lovers have known for ages."

"Yes?" Rowen prompted.

"The Romans called it Cupid, because it seems to come from outside. As if we had no choice. I don't know about you," he said, his eyes laughing, "but I didn't have any, right from the beginning. Why don't we sit on this couch, for Pete's sake? You invite me here and then expect me to stand up?"

"Invite you! You were down here as soon as you heard my key in the lock."

Dave nodded happily. "I watched the clock all afternoon. I feel like this place is ours. Do you mind?"

"That's the way I want you to feel!"

"What else do you want me to feel?" He slipped both hands beneath the jacket of her new spring suit and massaged her breasts suggestively, teasing her nipples into taut buds while his mouth devoured hers.

"I want you to feel everything," she answered simply when she had a chance.

"Feed Vicky, and let's try your new mattress again."

Rowen agreed promptly. She had never imagined that lovemaking could be so spontaneous or so much fun.

They coupled with delightful abandon, reaffirming with every touch and caress their commitment to each other. After ward, lying with her head cradled in the hollow of Dave's shoulder, she felt completely open to him, mind, soul and body.

"Dave . . ."

He grunted.

"I have to confess something."

He groaned, reading her hesitation as reluctance to ask a favor. "Let me guess! More furniture. You want me to be on hand to receive it."

"Yes, more will be coming, but it's something else."

He was tantalizing her, trailing the fingers of his free hand between her breasts, over the arch of her rib cage and across her bare belly.

Hair tickled her palm as her hand roamed across his chest.

"All right, what's the confession?" He moved her head from his shoulder and rose up on one elbow to look her in the face. "I suppose you've spent more than you could afford."

"No . . ." She giggled. "I haven't spent more than I can afford. Really."

"What, then?"

"I have two cats."

Dave let out a roar of laughter. "And you had the nerve to make me feel weird for keeping Harrison's kittens!"

"But that makes three for you!"

"So a two-cat owner looks down her nose at a three-cat owner?" He circled her ankle with one hand and tickled the sole of her foot. She shrieked protestingly.

"This is called the cartoonist's revenge." He nipped the end of each toe in turn.

She lay back, laughing helplessly.

Later, in Dave's apartment, eating spaghetti and meatballs, she told him that she would be moving in on the evening of the thirty-first.

"I'll help," Dave offered.

"I'm calling movers for my clothes and my books, but I'd like you to meet my relatives."

Her aunt and uncle understood that she wanted her own apartment, but if they asked to see it . . . With Dave along, they wouldn't ask. They'd wait to be invited.

During the following week Dave took delivery of a smart Swedish dining set. He helped Rowen unpack boxes of linens, china, expensive cookware and cutlery, enough glassware for a party and silverware.

"Looks like you bought everything the housewares department had to offer," he commented. "I don't want to criticize, but aren't you being a little extravagant?"

"I can afford it," she said blithely.

The wild way she spent money began to worry him. He determined to be very cautious about getting more deeply involved, but it was a little late for caution. He was already deeply involved. She had taken the apartment at his suggestion.

Then she moved in.

A routine was established from the first day. When she arrived home from work, Dave closed up shop, too. He and Clancy adjourned to her apartment. Soon the place was as familiar as his own. He did their shopping early in the morning so he and Rowen could fix dinner together. Afterward, if they didn't go out, they spent the evening in her cheerful living room. They spent the night in her cheerful bedroom. Dave had never been so happy or so comfortable.

They lived in a bubble of enchantment all through the month of April. Sundays they explored the city. They roamed the cavernous empty streets of the downtown area, checking out new buildings, craning their necks to discover architectural oddities on old ones. They worked their way uptown to the iron fronts of Soho.

"Vicky and Clancy must think we're out of our minds." Rowen laughed. Some instinct kept her from suggesting that they take the dogs to the country in her Mercedes station wagon. She kept it garaged a few blocks from the apartment, though she used it only infrequently to attend out-of-town book auctions with Horace.

The weather couldn't have been lovelier—the air cool, the sunshine sparkling. Weekend showers washed the streets and sidewalks.

When they dined out, Rowen scrupulously insisted on paying her share.

Dave's outlook began to change. He decided quite objectively that Rowen's happiness was more important than cartooning. He began to think of making a commitment to the future. That meant earning more money, taking temporary jobs. He listed his name with two agencies where he'd worked before.

Like it or not, he was a man who wanted commitment. What free soul would think of burdening himself with three cats and a dog? And a woman. Not that Rowen was a burden. She made life better in every way.

At the bookshop Rowen hung up the phone, hollow with disappointment. For the third time that week Dave had called to say he wouldn't be there for dinner. He was out on a free-lance job and would stay until he finished it.

"What about your own work?" she had exclaimed each time.

Each time he had told her that the next day would be soon enough to go back to work on what he was doing—rooms full of cats, kittens, and two demented dogs. The only people awaiting his cartoons were the editors of the magazine he had a contract with. He could do cartoons for them nights and weekends.

"You're not leaving any time for us!" Rowen pointed out when she got home that evening. "Almost the only time I've seen you this week is when we walk the dogs. If you'll be drawing this weekend, I'll barely see you then. . . ."

"You don't understand!" Dave said impatiently. "I have to take free-lance jobs when they're offered. I never know when they'll dry up."

"You said when I first met you that you didn't have to take free-lance jobs."

"Yeah, well . . . circumstances change." Dave looked uncomfortable.

"Are you . . ." Would he be insulted if she asked him if he was short of money?

"Am I what?"

"I wondered if you might be short of money."

"Looking to borrow some? I'm not surprised. You've been spending like a drunken sailor."

Rowen heard his grouchy tone with understanding. Even Dave couldn't work ten and twelve hours a day and stay cheerful. She didn't reply, because she didn't want to argue. Her silence didn't help.

Dave said, "I know you bought all that stuff because you wanted to make the place nice for me, sweetheart, and believe me, I love being there with you, but I love being with you anywhere—in my crummy pad, in a restaurant with a dog chewing my boot, even your aunt's fancy town house!"

"But what does my spending have to do with you?" she asked, puzzled.

He shrugged. "I thought I might pay half the rent. What the heck—I use the apartment, too."

"Dave!" She was so touched that her throat choked up. "It's no problem. Really!"

"Come off it, Rowen," he said roughly. "I've done

124

department-store layouts. I know what furniture costs. And dishes and stemware—crystal, no less! Those designer sheets alone probably set you back eighty dollars." His mouth covered hers as if to soften his harsh accusation.

She returned his kiss with a fervor born of relief. They stood on the dark street in a tight embrace. Clancy and Vicky wandered in a circle, wrapping their leashes around their owners' ankles.

Dave had been working to help her out with her finances! She could hardly believe it. As understanding sank in, her eyes filled with tears. He didn't want to take, he wanted to give!

And she'd been trying to figure how to help him out! She chuckled despite her watery eyes. This was the time to tell him how much money she really had. He'd be so relieved! He could go back to his own work without a worry.

He put her away from him so he could peer into her face. "What are you giggling about?"

She hesitated. He didn't sound in the best of moods, but when he understood . . .

"There's no problem about paying—honest!"

"Then you must have a lot more money than you earn at that measly bookshop."

"It's not measly!" she cried. "No more measly than your cartoons! That shop is known to collectors all over the country." She felt Dave draw a breath to argue, or apologize, and rushed on. "But, yes, I do have more money. You just assumed . . ."

"I've been meaning to ask how big that trust fund is." His tone told her that his mood had lightened. He planted a swift salute on her kiss-warmed lips.

They untangled the leashes and let the dogs forge ahead.

"So I'm in love with an heiress!" he said cheerfully. "How many millions, darling?"

Rowen drew a deep breath. "About two, at last count."

"You're kidding!" Dave pulled Clancy to a stop so suddenly that the hound's toenails rasped the sidewalk. He stared at Rowen. In the light of the streetlamp she read consternation on his face. Something in his stance or the tone of his voice tied her stomach in a knot.

"Isn't that lucky?" She spoke brightly.

"Two million dollars! You're putting me on." He laughed as if at a good joke.

"No, I'm not. The amount changes," she added vaguely. She had never expected him not to believe her.

He stared into her eyes. "You're not kidding! I want you to be, but you're not." He sounded withdrawn. For a time they walked in silence. "And I was calling you a waif," he mused. "You must have laughed yourself silly."

"I kept telling you I wasn't. But I didn't laugh. I was touched."

"Two million dollars!" he repeated in awe. "How do you keep track of it?"

"I don't. The trustees tell me what I can spend."

"And you're playing around with a bookstore?"

"I'm not playing, damn it! Horace is teaching me the business."

"Gee . . ." His words came painfully. "You wanted to know why I was working. . . .I took those free-lance jobs because I thought . . . maybe, if I had a few thousand in the bank as a backlog, we could work something out. Like . . . I don't know. . . . There's no use talking about it now." He looked so defeated that her heart seemed to stop. "I thought I wouldn't have to feel a full-time job breathing down my neck every time I didn't get a good check from the cartoons. And I wouldn't have to worry about being a burden if I got knocked over by a car, or something. I don't have health insurance, you know. Too expensive. And all the time . . ." Again he laughed. "You realize this blows everything?"

"Why should it?" she cried.

They were back in front of their building. He turned on her. "No wonder those bastards were all over you at the party! No wonder you were living on Sutton Place!"

"I don't live there now. I live here." To prove it, she took out her key and opened the door.

He followed her in.

He said, "I remember you laughed at me for my creative imagination." His voice sounded deep and dignified and furious. "You were right, weren't you? I imagined a pretty little waif who needed me to take care of her. And you let me go right on fantasizing. You should have told me, Rowen."

"I did tell you! I told you I had some money—"

"*Some money!*"

They reached her floor. She unlocked her door. Dave walked on.

"Aren't you coming in?" she choked.

"Not tonight." His voice was bitterly cold. "See you around."

"I thought you'd be excited! Look how free it makes us!"

He laughed hollowly. The last she saw of him were boots and blue jeans, disappearing up the steps.

She pushed open her door and followed Vicky inside. Leaning against the closed door, she waited for pain to follow disbelief.

The next day she was too proud and angry to telephone him. How dare he treat her like a leper because she'd been born lucky! Could you call it lucky? One man had married her for her money; the next guy turned his back on her because of it. Was it some kind of a curse? Other people managed to live happily with a fortune.

She brooded all day at work, hoping Dave would come to his senses and show up at her door when she got home. He didn't. She told herself that the breach was temporary. Since she heard no footsteps overhead when she returned home, she decided that he had gone out for the evening.

At last she could bear the loneliness no longer. She telephoned Celia in Boston. No answer. She kept trying. It was after eleven before Celia finally picked up the phone. Rowen told her what had happened and began to cry.

"Stop that!" Celia said sternly. "A man doesn't dump a woman because she's rich. He's nursing his pride, that's all. Give him time. He'll realize it's not so bad to fall in the gravy."

"Yes, but—" Rowen's voice broke as she began to cry again.

"Stop crying!" Celia ordered once more. "Dry your eyes and put on some makeup. Waylay him in the hall. You haven't committed a crime. You're not obliged to give a financial statement when you go to bed with a man."

Rowen choked on a laugh despite her sorrow. "Oh, Celia! You have such good sense! Thanks for making me feel better."

They talked for an hour, mostly about Celia's latest men. "Call me tomorrow night," she told Rowen at the end. "I'll be home sometime."

Rowen hung up, and her troubles descended again. She caught back a sob. She had all the next day to get through before she could confront Dave. She couldn't stay up listening for him any longer tonight. He might not come home until morning. That idea produced another sob.

I look terrible, she thought, studying her face in the bathroom mirror. If Dave knocked on my door now, I wouldn't answer.

She lay on the bed with a wet washcloth across her eyes. It wasn't easy to stop crying. Tears overflowed and ran down her temples.

Vicky came to the bedside, begging to be taken for her late-night walk. What if they met Dave with another woman? But Vicky had to go out. . . .

Rowen cringed all the way down the three flights. She met no one. The weight of her fear lifted as she pushed open the street door. And there he was! Alone, at least.

"Dave . . . ?"

He pushed by without a word.

She made Vicky's walk as short as possible. Upstairs she dialed Celia as if her life depended on it. Her friend's voice was sleepy, but Rowen was beyond caring.

"He won't speak to me! I met him downstairs. He wouldn't even look at me!"

"He may take a few days to come to his senses," Celia conceded. "But you can work it out. Keep reminding yourself there's no way a man can turn down your kind of money."

"You don't know him," Rowen said. She heard a smothered

yawn. Pride made her say, "Thanks a lot, Celia. I'm sorry I woke you."

"Call me tomorrow."

"I will if I have anything to say. I'm not calling long distance just to cry." She managed a laugh.

"You can afford it," Celia said thoughtlessly.

"Yes, I can! Good night." Suddenly enraged, Rowen dropped the receiver in its cradle. What an unfeeling remark! She was furious with Celia, and furious with herself for crying. And furious with Dave.

"The hell with them both!" she told Vicky.

Pride rescued her. Pride and anger. She went to work the next day with her head up, defiant. Beneath her poised exterior she might be raw and bleeding, but no one needed to know. That evening and the next, television kept her from thinking. Two agonizing days passed.

She was still too proud to telephone him, but during a weak moment she pushed a note under his door. It said in straightforward English that she hated not seeing him, and suggested they talk. No answer.

Now she knew Dave's flaw. He was secretly arrogant. He was full of self-satisfaction and pride, like a Victorian male. He wanted to dominate his world. He had to be the one who supplied the money, the protection, the approval, the advice.

How right she had been to be cautious about moving in with him! What would he have done in that case? Booted her out?

For a while she forgot her anger by asking herself how he would have behaved if she had actually been living in his apartment. He wouldn't have ordered her to move out. He was too kind-hearted for that. In fact, she knew she was exaggerating his flaw.

If we had been living together, she decided, he would have had to accept me—money and all. The thought brought a sour smile. Perhaps she should have been braver. The next thought followed logically. If we were married, the money would be ours jointly.

For some reason the idea of marriage to Dave didn't frighten her this time. The frightening thing now was that apparently he was never going to speak to her again.

She set her jaw. Now that she knew what she wanted, she was willing to bide her time.

Another day passed before she ran into him. She was late leaving for work the next morning and happened to open her door as he went by.

"Dave . . ." She put out a hand to halt him, but he paused of his own accord.

"Still here?" he asked brightly.

The blood left her face, but her eyes hungrily devoured his beloved features. "How long are you going to keep avoiding me?" she managed to say.

"Till you get tired of seeing how the other half lives. Go back to your own set, Rowen."

She recoiled, but recovered quickly. She had planned what to say when she got a chance. "Dave, what have I done that's so bad? You were the one who started everything. You insisted on sketching Vicky."

He had paused, head lowered. To keep from meeting her eyes! He knew that electric jolt would still flash between them!

"I'm sorry," he said, throwing her a brief glance. "It was my mistake." He walked on.

"There wasn't any mistake!" she called after him, stamping her foot.

She certainly wasn't going to move out of her newly furnished apartment! She locked her door and marched downstairs in his wake. Move back where? By her "own set" she supposed he meant the people at Celia's party. Well, she didn't have a set—she didn't want one!

Walking toward Madison Avenue, she decided that she had always been a loner. Dave's words hadn't stung; they simply didn't apply. For the first time in her life she was truly independent. She caught a flash of what Dave had tried to explain when she first met him. He had been proud of his self-sufficiency. Now she, too, was self-sufficient.

She recalled how she had once thought that if things went

wrong with Dave, she would pack her bags and run. How simpleminded that had been! She had her dog, her cats, her . . . home. Last week Horace had complimented her on her feel for rare books. Except for the day-and-night heartache, life was fine. She grimaced at the irony.

Surely Dave would see the foolishness of his stand. At times she was sure he must. At others she faced the possibility of defeat. He couldn't seem to see that money didn't mean a thing when it came to finding happiness. It was nothing but an obstacle!

She came home that evening to hear the kittens romping overhead on the bare floor. She missed them and she missed Dave. Her mouth sagged, and her eyes filled with tears that threatened to spill over. She brushed them away and stalked into the kitchen to feed her animals and pour herself a sherry.

At the ring of the telephone she jumped. Her heart seemed to stop. Her hand hovered over the receiver like a gambler hesitating over a card. Her hello came out as a croak.

"Rowen?" A male voice. Not Dave's.

"Oh, Stewart! Hello."

"Listen, I know it's last-minute, but would you have dinner with me?"

"What's the occasion?" After his bitter remark the last time, she hadn't expected to hear from him again, except in the course of his duties as her trustee.

"I'd like to see you, that's all."

Rowen drew a deep, painful breath. "I'd like to have dinner, Stewart. Do you want to meet me somewhere?"

"No, I have your new address in my file. I'll pick you up in, say, half an hour? Is that too soon? The fact is, I'm starving. I played racquetball at noon instead of eating lunch."

"Half an hour's fine. I'm on the third floor. Stewart, don't be shocked. The building's a walk-up."

After a moment of silence Stewart said, "Economizing?"

"Seeing how the other half lives. See you about seven."

Standing before her closet, she wished she'd said no. Stewart would want to know why she had chosen this abominable building. However, she was committed to going, and it would be nice to eat with someone instead of alone.

She slipped into a full-skirted rose cotton dress that had come from one of the exclusive shops near her bookstore. She added dangling silver earrings and a chunky necklace of carved bone and wood that had caught her fancy when she bought the dress. A glance at her appearance cheered her.

Then Stewart arrived, and she wished again that she had said no. The sight of him brought back poignantly the last time they had been out together—and had met Dave.

History seemed bound to repeat itself, because they met Dave on the stairs.

"This place!" Stewart was saying. "You're weird, Rowen!"

Dave waited for them to descend the stairs. He was wearing blue shorts with a white stripe down the side, a white shirt and blue running shoes. His thighs, with their covering of light brown hair, made Rowen close her eyes, remembering. Remembering the feel of them against her own thighs and how beautiful his whole body was. When she met his direct look, he gave a cool nod. Her insides seemed to disintegrate.

"Wasn't that your cartoonist?" Stewart asked.

She found her voice. "Yes, it was."

She was grateful that Stewart didn't pursue the subject.

They had finished dinner and were sipping liqueurs when he said suddenly, "So you took an apartment in the cartoonist's building. I gather things didn't work out?"

"What?" Rowen came close to spilling her *creme de menthe*.

"You and the cartoonist. Rowen . . ." He reached for her hand. "When are you going to come to your senses? I've been waiting, giving you time. I didn't expect you to get serious over that guy."

"Who said I was serious?" she asked, her voice brittle.

"I hope you're not, because I've been serious about you for a long time."

He was looking at her from under light brown brows, his eyes steady, his blond hair shining in the candlelight. She had always been fascinated by his clean-cut type, and had known other men and boys with similar facial structures. They looked great in tennis whites. But they never looked *real*. She tried to imagine Stewart chopping wood. Or diapering a baby. Doing anything ordinary people did.

"Rowen . . ." He captured her other hand so that she had to look into his eyes. "Rowen, marry me! We're the same sort of people. We know the kind of life we want. . . ."

"I don't love you," she said as gently as she could.

"You could learn! I'm faithful, I promise you—not like Skeffington. I've never been a woman chaser. We could have a great life—good apartment in the city, or a house in Westchester, if you prefer . . . sailing on weekends, skiing in the winter. I'm from your world, Rowen!"

Her heart twisted with the irony of it. Her grasp on his hands tightened to help her bear her painful thoughts. She didn't care about that world. Did he love her, or was she merely part of the bargain? She could imagine the cool, considerate relationship they would have, and her heart rebelled.

"I'll think about it," she said at last. Recalling her aunt and uncle's marriage, which had never seemed terribly passionate to her, she added, "It might work." What was the use of pursuing a hopeless dream? If Dave was stupid enough to turn away from her, to let money stand in the way of their love . . .

How could he be so foolish? Her anger returned. Maybe seeing her with Stewart would wake him up to what he was missing. Did he care?

She sighed. "Right now I'm pretty happy with my life the way it is."

That wasn't quite a lie. Somehow she would coax Dave to come back.

The next evening, when she arrived home from work, she heard Dave coming down the stairs. By the time they met in front of her door her heart was beating a wild tattoo. She gave him a wary glance. Would he freeze her out again? No! This time his eyes were bright with menace as he bore down on her.

"You didn't waste any time getting back to your wealthy friends," he gritted in a tone so ominous that she could hardly adjust her mind to what he was saying. "What did your lawyer friend think of your apartment?"

The question awoke the sullen fury in Rowen's heart. "He asked me if I was economizing!"

"What did I tell you? Fixing up this apartment was nothing but an eccentric caper for you."

"It was not!" Rowen stamped her foot. Her eyes filled with tears of frustration. "You two should get acquainted—you think just alike!"

"When is he going to carry you off, back to the elegant life where you belong?" Dave demanded fiercely. "I'd like to know, so I can settle down and do my own work."

"He's not going to carry me anywhere!"

"Why not? You were having an affair with him before I came along, weren't you? Before you decided to have a little adventure in the world of the middle class." Dave's eyes narrowed to slits, the blue gleaming like cold steel. Rowen could hardly believe he was the same person. Who would have guessed that her easygoing cartoonist could become so inexorable and angry?

"I was not having an affair with Stewart! It also happens he's not wealthy."

Dave raised a disbelieving eyebrow. "You mean not as rich as you are? Is that why he didn't take his eyes off you for a minute at that party? He wants you *and* your money, Rowen. By the way, you answered one question for me—how your friend Celia could snag so many unattached men. Obviously she's rich, too. She didn't pretend not to be. You were the one who lied."

"I did not!" His attack was leaving her short of breath. Other, darker emotions swirled between them. "I never pretended I was poor!" she cried. She recalled Celia's remark. "Where does it say I had to give you a financial statement?"

"You told me you were house-sitting—and you knew what I

thought." His voice dropped. "You're out of my league, Rowen. Way out."

"What league? This isn't baseball!" She glared at him.

"Do I have to spell it out? You can't fit into my life."

"Try me."

He shook his head. "You would run back to your rich friends the first time we had a disagreement. Like you did last night. But let me give you some advice about your friend Stewart. He's after your money."

"I'm glad you brought that up." Rowen took a deep breath, resentful of his ridiculous paternalism. "Am I supposed to spend my life alone because Stewart or someone else doesn't think it's dishonorable to love a woman with money?"

"It's the money he loves!"

"Are you saying I'm not lovable?"

"God knows you are!" Dave's voice rose with the intensity of his feelings. "But that bastard has his greedy eyes on your fortune. I could tell from talking to him five minutes. I didn't understand his attitude then, because I didn't know you were loaded. Is he pretending he loves you?" He reached for her wrist, his eyes fierce.

"What do you care?" Rowen pulled away and turned to unlock her door.

"I care, believe me! But there's nothing I can do about it." His eyes lost their fire and became veiled. He stepped around her and ran down the stairs.

Dave had felt himself melting in the face of her disappointment. If he'd stayed any longer, he'd have carried her into the bedroom and forgotten all about the damned money.

He bought the frozen dinner he'd been going down to get and took it back upstairs. He walked into his apartment and felt stifled.

"Clance, let's get out of here!" He took the hound's leash from its hook.

The May evening was so beautiful that it tore at his heart. It seemed crazy not to be sharing it with Rowen. His mouth twisted with bitter regret. A May evening was about the best he had to share, while she . . . she had two million dollars. She didn't need anybody to share anything.

And he couldn't let her share that money with him! A man had to have some pride. If pride made him a male chauvinist, he couldn't help it; it was bred in his bones.

He could contribute nothing to a marriage with her. Nothing.

He had been on a seesaw ever since he found out about her money. He couldn't have her; he had to have her. More important, nobody should have her who wasn't worthy of her. Definitely not Stewart.

He began to think about his upcoming trip to Missouri. He had never mentioned it to Rowen. He hadn't wanted to think about leaving her, let alone talk about it. Now . . . he wanted to leave her less than ever. Anything could happen while he was gone. God, she might take him up on the taunt he had made tonight and move out!

He had planned to borrow Mel's car and drive to Missouri with Clancy. He had expected to ask Rowen to feed his cats. He could hardly do that now.

On the other hand, why not? She was a friend and neighbor, wasn't she? The real point was that she couldn't do anything crazy like move out if she had the responsibility for his animals and apartment. He could leave Clancy, too, if she'd agree. That would really tie her down. He could fly to Missouri and back, and not be gone as long.

My God, he thought, here I am trying to get her out of my life, and I can't contemplate leaving her for seven days.

Nothing could happen to her, he told himself sternly, that her money wouldn't take care of. Except Stewart. She mustn't get involved with that turkey.

He turned and started back home. He refused to think about whether his decision made sense in the long run. He knew only that it felt right. If Rowen would agree. . . .

"Clancy, you'll look after her." The idea of Clancy as a guard dog almost made him smile.

He was within a block of home when he saw her walking

Vicky. Her back was to him; she was returning home, too. Seeing her unexpectedly like that made his emotions churn worse than ever. It was delightful, exciting, then a letdown. She could never be his.

She was wearing a loose poplin jacket that hid her delightfully small waist and the flare of her hips, but he knew the shape of her as well as he knew his own. Better. He drew a sharp, painful breath when he thought of the beautiful hours he had spent touching her, caressing every intimate part of her.

He put the memory out of his mind and approached light-footedly, cautioning himself to keep a leash on his feelings. What he wanted now was a commitment from her that was for her own good.

The way Rowen's heart behaved when she turned and saw Dave and Clancy walking toward her made her feel a little sick. He had told her not an hour before that he wanted her out of his life. How could she be so thrilled simply to lay eyes on him again?

She stood tensely, waiting for him to walk right by. Instead he stopped. When she dared to turn her head in his direction, she saw that he was looking contrite.

"Rowen, I owe you an apology for what I said upstairs a while ago. What you do with your life is really none of my business. I hope we can still be friends. And neighbors."

"Y-yes," she stammered. The idea sounded deadly.

"I . . . well, I may need to ask you a favor."

Rowen raised her eyebrows. She was too taken aback by a sudden rush of satisfaction to find words. He needed her! The last of her resentment fled.

"Sure, Dave. Anything I can do." She spoke flatly to hide her pleasure.

"It's like this. . . ." He stood rubbing his jaw while Clancy sniffed around a two-foot square of impatiens. Two passing women looked Dave up and down with obvious yearning.

In the fading light he looked wonderfully virile in his chinos and tight-fitting T-shirt. Rowen's mind leapt wildly to produce a grassy spring meadow in the dusk, and Dave cavorting faunlike and naked. She tossed her head to dismiss the fantasy and urged him to say what was on his mind.

He strolled on, tugging Clancy away from the flowers as they headed back toward their building. It seemed easier for Dave to talk when they were walking side by side.

"My folks are celebrating their fortieth wedding anniversary at the end of this month. More than anything they want all us kids to be there. The problem is, I can't fly with Clancy. He went into shock and darn near died when I flew him to New York." Dave threw up his hands. "The kennels I checked out are impossible for a dog Clancy's size."

"So you want me to look after him?"

"Would you? I know it's a big favor. . . ."

"I'd be happy to look after Clancy, and the cats, too. Dave . . ." Rowen forced him to meet her gaze. "You must know I'm glad to do you a favor. How soon are you going?" Her joy in helping him sagged at the thought that he was leaving town.

"A week from Saturday, probably. The big shindig's planned for that Sunday." He gave a rueful smile. "Pets are great until you try to go someplace."

Rowen was struck by an idea. "Would you want to drive?" she asked tentatively. "You could take my station wagon, and take Clancy with you. Not that I won't be happy to look after him. . . .It's just a thought."

"You have a station wagon? You never told me that, either!"

"The subject never came up!"

He paced in silence for so long that Rowen feared she had made him angry again.

At length he said, "You know how to heap coals of fire on a man's head, don't you?"

"What do you mean?"

"Returning good for evil. It's from the Bible."

He was silent once more. She kept her fingers crossed. She longed to do something for him. That was what love was about. Perhaps what angered Dave was that he thought he couldn't do anything for her. But he could! Not financially, but in so many other ways.

"I only use it for business" she explained nervously. "When Horace and I go to book auctions. I don't like driving in town."

"Won't you need it?"

The question meant he was considering her offer!

"Nothing is coming up in the next few weeks."

At the door of their building he said without thinking, "Too bad you can't come with me."

Rowen came to a standstill. "Do you mean that?"

Had he meant it? He had spoken on impulse, but he couldn't retract his words.

"I could get off for a few weeks! Horace can mind the store."

"Are you serious?" Dave halted in the doorway, aghast to hear his impulsive remark taken up so quickly. That, he reflected, was the difference between rich people and poor people. Rich people could go anywhere, anytime. On the other hand, if it meant that they could be together . . .

"It would mean taking all the animals," he warned, torn between dissuading her and wanting her with him. "We'd have to camp out. A motel wouldn't let us in the front door with such a menagerie."

He held the door while Rowen and the dogs marched in.

"How do you feel about car camping?" he asked on the way upstairs. "Have you ever done it? We could get a campground guide and figure out where we can stop each night. The animals will love it more than being cooped up in one room. I have a hammock, and we can make room for you to sleep in the station wagon."

"Wouldn't we sleep together?"

Dave groaned. "Rowen, your romantic fling of rich girl–poor boy is over. If we go, we go as friends, not lovers. You have to understand that. Maybe when you see how people without a fortune live, you'll be ready to end this excursion into poverty."

She bit her lip. There was no point in arguing. "I'd still like to go," she said stubbornly.

Dave paused at her door. "You'll get to see parts of the country you've never seen before. I'll pay for the gas, naturally. Campgrounds, too. We'll talk more about it next week. I'll figure out when we'll need to leave and let you know."

She had hoped he would walk into her apartment as naturally as he would have a week before. She was too proud to invite him and risk being turned down.

Going upstairs, Dave cautioned himself to be guarded and sensible, but his spirits soared. The prospect of having Rowen at his side for a trip halfway across the country made him want to bound up to the roof and cheer. At the end of the trip, he told himself sternly, Rowen would understand why a cartoonist and a millionaire couldn't walk hand-in-hand into the sunset. His background, for Pete's sake, was modest middle class. Barely that. He probably didn't earn in a year what she spent in a month.

He scowled. His family had pride and ethics. Poor but honest. He decided he was being self-righteous and smiled sourly. If only she didn't have *quite* so much money . . .

How much could you stomach? he asked himself. *One million? Half a million?* There was no answer. She had it, and that was that.

"You understand we're going as friends," Dave reminded her sharply the night he came down to make detailed plans for the trip.

Rowen had laid out a buffet meal from an expensive delicatessen—roast chicken, potato salad, an elegant tomato and zucchini salad. She had discovered that without cooking at all people could make out very well among restaurants, delis and East Side supermarkets. It was nothing like sharing the fun of making meals with Dave, but she wouldn't starve.

Actually, she was putting on weight. If she went to a good restaurant and picked at the food, the waiter took a fatherly interest in her appetite. It was easier to eat than find an excuse for leaving her plate scarcely touched.

Judging from the supplies Dave listed as necessary for their trip, it sounded as though they might get back to cooking.

"Over a campfire?" she asked in amazement. "Like pioneers?"

"Not quite." Dave laughed. "I won't expect you to make bread."

"This will be the most adventurous thing I've ever done," Rowen said doubtfully.

"I thought you'd sailed a lot."

"Oh, yes. But if we went to the Bahamas or Bermuda, one of the crew cooked."

It was Dave's turn to say, "Oh!"

9

They set out the following Tuesday, heading across the George Washington Bridge and planning to drive through New Jersey into Pennsylvania. They made a pact not to rush. The animals needed to stretch their legs often, and Rowen felt that the journey couldn't last long enough.

The backseat had been folded down to make space for the dogs during the day, and for Rowen's new sleeping bag at night. Dave had bought a rabbit cage in which Ms. Harrison and the kittens reposed. Rowen's Himalayans were confined to their carriers. She planned to let them loose in the car at rest stops, or walk them on leashes.

She bubbled with happiness. As they crossed the Hudson River, leaving Manhattan behind, she looked over her shoulder.

"I've never done anything so crazy!" she said with a chuckle.

"Stick with me, kid," Dave answered without thinking.

"I'd like to."

He heard the wistfulness in her tone and cursed himself for being an insensitive brute. To make up for it, he patted her knee.

"Now you're really gonna see how the other half lives," he said jocularly. "As soon as we get through Pennsylvania, I think we'll head off onto the old U.S. highways. They're only used locally now. It's fun to go through the towns if you're not in a hurry."

Rowen feasted her eyes on Dave's profile and exulted. Except for two dogs and five cats, she had him all to herself. She could hardly keep from touching him. Her palm itched to curve over the bulge of muscle on the arm beside her, to stroke his forearm with its dusting of golden hairs. She longed to trail her fingers across his sturdy masculine wrist, and wanted to slip her arms around his waist and hug him. Or, as that would impede his driving, run one fingertip down the slant of his straight nose. But touching was taboo if they were to be merely friends.

Neither that nor anything else was going to dim her pleasure in this trip. She would be with him, day and night, for seventy-two hours or more. She had the station wagon to thank. Money—considering the things it could buy—wasn't a bad thing to have, no matter what Dave's principles dictated.

She began to think about the clothes she had packed, wondering if she had selected right. She had chosen the simplest clothes in her wardrobe, including three pairs of jeans.

The sun was still hours from the horizon when they arrived at the wooded campground Dave had picked. As he explained, making camp in the dark was impossible. The grounds were part of a state forest. Rowen looked from the car in fascination at the nearly empty circle of campsites. Scattered among the trees were cement tables.

She stepped out of the car and stared around in astonishment. "Is this all there is?"

"What more do we need? That tire rim serves as a fire pit. The toilets are over there, and probably cold showers." Dave pointed to a small wooden building.

Uneasily Rowen set out the cat carriers. Used to a roof overhead, both cats crouched lower. Rowen understood their reluctance. However, the dogs had leapt from the back of the wagon as soon as Dave opened the door and were now circling the area, busily sniffing.

Together Rowen and Dave set out the rabbit cage. On the far side of the circle were a motor home and a small house trailer, both apparently unoccupied at the moment. From far away came the sigh of traffic on the highway. Otherwise, the silence was deafening.

"Where is everybody?" she asked, her voice low.

"Still traveling, probably. It's Tuesday; there may not be too many people wanting to camp."

"I meant *here*. Who runs this place?"

"State foresters. If they don't come around to collect the fee, there'll be a box to put it in by the bulletin board over there. Want to walk over and see what the board says?"

"I'll wait for you."

"All right. Let's get the animals fed." Dave took dog and cat food from their supply and began opening cans. Rowen stood by, feeling helpless.

"What can I do?" she asked at last.

Dave threw her an amused glance. "See if you can lay hands on the dishpan and the cooking gear. The matches are there, too. Then you can build a fire."

"I can? With what?" Rowen looked wildly to the right and left.

"Sticks, twigs, fallen branches. Walk around; see if you can find some. Most campers don't bother with wood. They use camp stoves."

"Why aren't we?"

"Because we don't have one." Dave's tone was short.

Rowen sighed, partly from weariness and partly from confusion.

She tried Dave's patience and her own by being unable to find the required items among the carefully stowed shopping bags and suitcases.

That first evening it was miraculous to see Dave turn empty woods and a cement slab on legs into a cozy pocket of civilization. Feeling bewildered and useless, Rowen sat on the cement bench and watched. She was grateful when he began telling her what to do—pick up sticks, fetch water, cut up vegetables for a salad.

Dave heated a can of stew in an iron skillet. When the stew boiled, he spread a layer of biscuit dough over the top, popped on an iron cover and set it aside to bake. They took Ms. Harrison out for a walk. Inside the cage the kittens tumbled playfully.

As the sun disappeared behind the trees, the dogs grew tired of exploring and came to sit inside the enchanted circle. Dave produced a tablecloth and suggested that Rowen set the table while he opened the wine.

There they were, in the middle of the woods, alone together with all their needs at their fingertips.

"No wonder people love camping!" Rowen exclaimed.

Dave raised his glass, and his eyes crinkled. She drew a deep, happy breath. She hadn't seen that amused expression on his face for a long time.

"This is like when we first met," she said gleefully. "Just us. No complications."

He nodded, drinking his wine in silence. "Haven't you ever been camping—really camping?"

Slowly she shook her head. "Summer camps, but that's not what you mean, is it? I've never backpacked, or slept outside."

Dave told her about coon hunting with his uncles and neighbors when he was a boy. "Mostly it was an excuse for the men to sit under a tree all night and spin yarns. And drink and listen to the hounds bay."

"Did they kill the raccoons?"

"Yeah. That part wasn't so pleasant, but I was ashamed to admit I was squeamish and stay home. *Sensitive* was not a complimentary word where I grew up." Dave slid out from the table. "I think the food's ready."

The canned stew and quick bread, on a plastic plate, with the smell of wood smoke in her nostrils, tasted as good as any dinner Rowen had ever eaten. They washed the dishes in water heated over the campfire and packed up. Dave strung his hammock between two trees and unrolled his sleeping bag inside the mesh cocoon. Light still lingered, so they shut the cats in the car and set out to explore a rutted road that led off among the trees, stopping first to deposit their camping fee in the locked box.

"Honor system," Dave explained.

That's what I'm on, Rowen thought. I'm on my honor not to touch him or be anything but aloof. How long, she wondered, would he hold out? Dinner out in the woods had been fine, but now she found herself thinking wistfully of a nice double bed in a motel, with hot showers and a toilet only steps away.

"Will we go to a motel if it rains?" she asked.

Dave grinned at her. "Wishing for a roof already?"

She reached for his hand and then thought better of it. "How do you know some ax murderer isn't going to attack us during the night?"

"Because we're out in the middle of nowhere. There are no ax murderers around. Trust me."

She trusted him, but she got very little sleep. She lay awake listening for stealthy footsteps. Twice she was on the verge of begging Dave to join her in the station wagon, but the warm bulk of Vicky curled against her helped control her fear. If anybody came around, the dogs would bark. Clancy was outside, under Dave's hammock.

When the birds began their early-morning chorus, Rowen opened her eyes to gray light filtering through the trees. She felt as if she'd been awake all night.

"Maybe you're right," she confessed when she was dressed and shivering over the most welcome cup of coffee she'd ever tasted.

"What about?" Dave was disgustingly cheerful. He had actually whistled while he built a fire and fed the animals.

"I'm not tough enough to be poor."

"I never said that!"

"No, but that's what this is, isn't it? You're trying to show me up. We're not staying in motels because you can't afford it. I checked it out, Dave. First-class motels take animals if you pay enough."

Dave gave her a look that mingled sympathy with tolerance. "Finish your coffee. We'll stop for breakfast at the first likely place. Things will look brighter then. This is supposed to be fun!"

Rowen washed her face in the cold water of the ladies' room. She had spent the night in jeans and a shirt because she'd been afraid to be caught undressed if trouble started. Now she felt icky. On a boat the facilities, though cramped, were available. She considered going to the nearest airport and flying back to New York, with Vicky and the cats in regulation crates, but she couldn't bear the thought of Dave's triumph and secret contempt.

Instead, his expression was bemused when she admitted her fears over breakfast.

"Sweetheart, there's absolutely nothing to be afraid of. Dangerous lunatics don't go camping. In a couple of days you'll be used to sleeping out. I've made this trip before, you know. Nothing's ever happened."

"Who with?" she asked quickly. "Your Missouri girl friend, I suppose."

"No, she preferred to fly."

Rowen knew there was nothing more futile than being jealous of someone's past, but she couldn't help deriving a spurt of satisfaction from hearing that Karen had disappointed Dave in this as well as other ways. She immediately made up her mind to learn to enjoy camping.

"How did you sleep?" she asked, turning away from her self-concern.

"Fine! Great!"

So much for the idea that he might find the hammock uncomfortable and join her in the back of the wagon.

"Of course," Dave amended, "after the city, it takes me a night or two to get used to the silence." He felt an almost irresistible urge to reach out and touch her—smooth her hair or squeeze her hand. She looked so defenseless sitting there eating scrambled eggs and toast—on his orders. Breakfast—that was one of the meals she skimped on. He had decreed that hearty breakfasts were to be one of the mainstays of the trip.

Had he been a beast? Would she be in discomfort all morning from a rebellious stomach? He wanted to assure her that he had her well-being at heart.

"Rowen . . ." She looked up. He evaded the depths of her brown eyes by focusing on her parted lips. He clenched his hands. He wanted to kiss her and promise her that they'd have a great time.

"Yes?"

He hauled his gaze away and stared out the window. He'd forgotten what he had meant to say. The sight of a truck with an Ohio plate put words in his mouth.

"Once we get out of Pennsylvania, we'll angle south toward the Ohio River. You'll like it, I promise."

"I'll try." She gave him a look from under her dark lashes that took his breath away. Did she know how seductive she had looked at daybreak, still half asleep, her brown eyes soft?

They took turns driving, stopping every couple of hours for coffee or at a roadside park to let the dogs run. They left the interstate, and Dave got a kick out of pulling into service stations that sold diesel fuel in the small towns they went through. The attendants didn't often see a diesel Mercedes station wagon, especially not one filled with animals and camping gear. He began picturing an old jalopy filled with dogs. The beginning of a cartoon was there somewhere.

They wended their way through the towns along the river to a state fishing lake among wooded hills. The campground was popular. Rowen found the easy friendliness of the other vacationers far more reassuring than the empty woods of the night before.

Children came scampering at the sight of the dogs and cats. Rowen was torn between enjoying their sociability and foolishly missing the previous night's exclusive solitude. She sat at the picnic table taking in everything—camping vehicles, people, scenery.

"I feel like I just flew in from Mars," she told Dave. "A stranger in my own country."

"You won't after this trip," Dave assured her.

"I think I'm going to love it, Dave. Thank you for bringing me along."

Dave looked at her shining eyes and felt a glow of pleasure. Then he remembered that she wasn't supposed to like it. The idea had been for her to recognize the gulf between his way of life and hers. She was supposed to realize that her fortune made her inalterably different from these people.

The third night set the seal on the failure of Dave's plans. A friendly group at the next campsite invited them for popcorn and a sing-along around the campfire. It was a big family— grandparents, married children with families of their own, aunts, uncles, cousins, nephews, nieces. They had guitars and song sheets. They sang and ate. Rowen sang, too, looking happier than Dave had ever seen her.

"You fit right in," he said as they groped their way back through the shadows.

"Wasn't it lovely? One of the best experiences of my life. I'll never forget it. What would it be like to belong to a family like that? I felt for a little while . . ." Her voice faltered. ". . . as if I did belong."

A lump in Dave's throat made it impossible to answer. He wanted to take her in his arms and tell her that she belonged to him, but it couldn't be. He thought of his brothers and sisters, the fun they had had growing up, the fun they would have when they got together this time. He had counted on Rowen's seeing how different his background was from hers. It hadn't occurred to him that she might see it as something to be envied.

He had trouble falling asleep. He lay listening to the night sounds of the camp and beyond. Off in the timbered hills a fox barked. A farm dog heard it and went into a frenzy.

Why was he lying alone in a hammock when Rowen lay only

steps away? He knew she was wearing a short satin nightgown over her new, fuller curves. His hands burned to touch her delectable flesh beneath the satin. He sat up, rubbing his palms together, and considered taking a walk, perhaps a plunge in the lake. Before he could reject the coldness of the lake water for the cocoonlike warmth of Rowen's sleeping bag, he made himself stand up. The cool grass beneath his bare feet brought him back to reality.

His scruples, his morals, everything he had learned, cried out against being supported by a woman. He had wanted a woman who was financially independent, but hell! He sat on the night-cooled bench of the picnic table and thought about it. He had gotten what he wanted.

There was no way he could accept it. No way! He shouldn't have brought her; he knew that now. Shaking his head, he climbed back into the hammock. He deserved to suffer.

They reached their destination Saturday morning. They could have arrived the night before by driving a few hours longer, but Dave had delayed, wanting to be alone with Rowen for another night. Even if he didn't allow himself to touch her, he could enjoy her complete attention, the carefree mood of their adventure.

Driving up the lane to the house, he noticed that the wide lawn was trim and the farmyard neat. The wave of pride and nostalgia that swept over him made him laugh, because this wasn't the way he remembered his home. When he was growing up, the place had been untended and overrun, the focus of seven busy lives. Now it looked like exactly what it was: the well-kept residence of a retired couple.

That view soon changed. A pack of children heard the car and came screaming. "Uncle Dave! Uncle Dave!" He forgot about the new neatness in the joy of homecoming.

Five youngsters tugged at the doors. Dave recognized his sister's two youngest, and the three belonging to his brothers. He introduced them to Rowen and let the dogs out. A brother and a brother-in-law materialized.

Rowen felt pleasantly overwhelmed as she was swirled into the vortex of the group. In the midst of the welcoming hubbub she met Dave's parents and was shown the room she would share with the teen-age daughters of one of Dave's sisters. Her cats were installed in the bedroom with their cat pan and water. It was obvious that once the cats emerged from under the beds, the children would be carrying them all over the house.

Rowen was made to feel welcome. The sister nearest in age to Dave lost no time in saying, "We were all so glad when Dave wrote he was bringing a new girl friend. Karen kept him dancing on a string for so long."

Before she could confide further, a child ran in shrieking that another uncle had arrived, and Rowen was hurried downstairs.

The whole weekend went like that—constant interruptions and excitement. Brothers, sisters, in-laws, all talked spiritedly, though some of them met almost daily. There were always at least two conversations going on. Rowen went to bed each night exhausted from trying to hear everything. In the midst of the goings-on meals got cooked, dishes washed and children kept track of.

Mealtimes were sheer heaven, Rowen thought. The adults sat at the long, old-fashioned dining table with all its leaves called into service. The children were fed at two smaller tables. After grace the chatter began. Inevitably some incident out of the past would come up, and they would be off, telling stories about this one or that one, shouting back and forth and laughing to bring the house down. Rowen had never heard so much laughter. Occasionally they ribbed Dave about New York. She watched the youngsters enviously, wondering what it would be like to grow up in the bosom of a big family, wondering if they appreciated it.

"They will when they look back," Dave said when she mentioned it. He had invited her for a walk across the pasture to the creek to see if the water was warm enough for swimming. She had anticipated an hour alone with Dave, but she was soon disillusioned. His whistle to Clancy might have been the notes of the Pied Piper. Clancy, Vicky, two nieces and two nephews came trotting. Rowen's disappointment melted when the little girls slipped their hands into hers, confident of their welcome.

The love with which this family surrounded its members was almost tangible. Rowen didn't think Dave realized its worth. And he thought he had nothing to offer her? She felt like a beggar, standing on the fringe, hoping to be invited in.

"As you see, a big family has drawbacks, too," he was saying. "No privacy."

Rowen smiled wistfully. "Want to trade places?"

Dave looked off across the fields, his eyes narrowed. "You can always get married and have a big family."

"Not if I don't start soon."

He returned his gaze to her, his eyes thoughtful. "Is that what you want, a big family?"

"What I want first is a loving husband," she said bluntly. She and Dave were the only adults without the legal right to share a bed. The setup bothered her a little. She hoped it bothered Dave a lot.

The boys came running to announce that they had found a coyote's den—perhaps. That ended that conversation.

The Archers's open house for neighbors and friends went on all Sunday afternoon and evening. Toward the end Dave pulled Rowen outside into the darkness.

"I haven't had you to myself in days." He surprised her with a hungry kiss.

"You're very friendly," she teased when she had caught her breath.

"I'm having trouble living up to my good intentions. Have you seen enough of Middle America to realize how different you and I are?"

"No."

Dave sat on the steps of the side porch and dragged her down beside him. "No? Darn it, Rowen, I brought you to Missouri so you'd understand." Under his light tone she sensed that he was serious.

"I understand one thing, Dave. When I see all the love your family has for one another, I realize you're the one who's wealthy, not me. Dave . . ."

"Here you are, you two!" Dave's older sister stepped onto the porch. "Dave, Mrs. Alvernon is ready to go home. Would you mind taking her? Your car's the only comfortable one available."

"Rowen's car," Dave corrected. He stood up—with relief, Rowen felt. The conversation wasn't going the way he wanted. It might be her car, but he carried the keys, and he didn't ask her to go with him.

She sat on the dark porch and watched the car pull out. Despite the fact that Dave hadn't invited her to go along, a sense of contentment stole over her. A few moments alone were pleasant when she could end her solitude at any time and return to the party.

What a warm, wholesome family! She saw no envy among them, or resentment. They enjoyed being together.

Rowen knew with a sudden ache that she wanted to belong, too. The idea of marrying Dave no longer frightened her. She knew him so well now, knew his background, his relatives. He had character and principles, and she loved him deeply.

Did he love her enough to abandon his false pride?

Three days later Dave and Rowen and their carful of animals left for New York.

"I don't feel I can take more time off," he explained in answer to his mother's objections. "Rowen has to get back, too. She has a shop to run."

"I love my family," he said when they were on the road, "but I think I'm becoming a crusty bachelor. I'm sick and tired of kids underfoot."

Rowen was silent. He had all the answers—*his* answers, anyway.

The rain began late Saturday afternoon in western Pennsylvania. Rowen was driving when the first drops hit the windshield. Dave seemed to be dozing. If the rain kept up, he wouldn't be able to sleep in his hammock! They were driving into it; she couldn't believe her luck.

The cozy dryness inside the car, the wet world outside, had a lulling effect. She began to dream of a motor home large enough for her and Dave—and the animals—to take a cross-country jaunt, staying at happy campgrounds as long as they wanted to.

Then the rain stopped. Dave woke up when she pulled into the parking lot of a roadside restaurant.

"It was raining a few miles back," she told him. "Maybe we ought to take a motel tonight. If you're short of money—"

"No motels," he growled, still half asleep and looking as cuddly as a small boy. "We set out to camp, so we camp."

"Okay." She made an elaborate pretense of not caring. This was their last night together. If he could spend eight nights with her, four going, four coming back, and not make love, she was defeated anyway. Whatever electrical charge that had flashed between them was dead.

The campground was nearly empty. Dave disclosed that he had put steaks and fresh ice in the cooler to celebrate their last night on the road. He set about cooking while Rowen tossed a salad. She was surprised and touched when a chilled bottle of champagne made its appearance.

Darkness hadn't quite descended by the time they sat down to enjoy the meal. The coals of the fire made a warm glow. The steak was excellent, and the champagne an amusing, sophisticated accent.

At the end of the meal Rowen said, "It's been a wonderful trip, Dave." Darkness had closed around them, and they were drinking coffee. "Thank you for everything." She laid her hand on his shoulder and kissed his cheek. Her lips still felt the coolness of his freshly shaven cheek as she gathered up her nightgown and robe and headed for the ladies' room.

"No point in crying now," she told herself sternly. "You'll have time for that in New York. Something might happen yet." No stars twinkled above the trees; the sky was overcast.

She woke to a crack of thunder loud enough to end the world. A gust of wind shook the station wagon. In the brief flashes of lightning that followed she saw leaves and twigs hurled across the ground. Vicky whined and hid her head under the sleeping bag.

Where was Dave? Between flashes the night was black.

As if at a signal, rain thundered on the roof. Hastily Rowen slid out of the sleeping bag and closed the side window. She raised the top half of the tailgate to peer out. Water poured through the crack overhead, so cold on her bare shoulders that her teeth chattered. She pulled the window shut and tried to see through the night.

What was happening to Dave?

She fumbled for the flashlight and switched it on in time to light up his blurred face outside in the darkness. His sodden sleeping bag was bundled in his arms. His shorts and T-shirt clung wetly to his body.

He had the tailgate open before Rowen could reach for the handle and scrambled in beside her, shivering uncontrollably. Clancy jumped in after him and promptly shook himself, spraying the whole interior with icy drops.

Rowen shrieked. With an oath Dave ordered Clancy to sit and closed the tailgate.

Brrrrr!"

Rowen giggled weakly. "Thank God you're all right! I was worried."

"It's only rain. *Cold* rain!"

She could feel him shaking. "We'll have you dry in a minute," she promised, fumbling for the towel she carried in her dressing case. "Strip off your wet clothes."

"Yes, ma'am." She felt him wriggling out of his garments, then he snatched the towel. She could hear him rubbing briskly. She plunged a hand into her suitcase, found her nubby terrycloth bath sheet and wrapped it around his shoulders.

"That's better!" he exclaimed, squeezing her fingers. "I woke up furious at you for pouring water on me, but it kept coming. I've got pajamas somewhere . . ." He fumbled in his suitcase.

155

Rowen unzipped her sleeping bag and spread it out.

"Move onto this," she suggested, enjoying a surge of excitement. They were not destined to sleep apart this night.

"Your invitation's accepted." Dave's voice was raw with wanting. "Oh, Rowen . . ."

He cupped her face like a chalice, and she felt his lips covering her cheeks and eyes with kisses. With a groan he took her mouth in all-consuming possession and drank its sweetness.

Wild excitement raced through her body. She burst into flames of desire, heightened by the knowledge that Dave, too, was charged with passion.

She opened her lips to him and felt his tongue drive deeply and promisingly into the dark richness of her mouth. She lay half beneath him, his arms binding her, body to body, flesh to flesh. She strained against him, holding him with all her strength while shivers of anticipation swept her.

Dave ended the kiss with a gasp and buried his face in her neck. "I can't keep away from you. I tried, but it's no good."

Rowen felt a thrill of pure gratitude to whatever genes had combined to make her desirable to Dave.

His lips traced a trail of adoring kisses across her cheek and down her throat to the sensitive spot above her collarbone. Her fingers fluttered across his back and down his lean sides, exploring him, loving the feel and shape of him, caressing every part of his body that she could reach.

His hands found the narrow straps of her dainty gown and bared her shoulders and then her breasts. Her body went taut with exquisite delight as his tongue brushed the pulsating tips. She grasped his head, running her fingers through his tousled hair while her body throbbed with expectation.

At length he raised his head to say, "I love you, Rowen. Never doubt that."

She murmured a response while running her tongue sensuously along the corded muscles of his strong masculine neck.

Dave shuddered and groaned. "Stop! You're driving me crazy!" He rolled away from her. She nipped his neck in retaliation.

"I need you, Rowen. God, how I need you tonight. Do you need me at all?"

"Oh, Dave! How can I convince you?"

"You can't convince me, because it's all wrong, but I want you so much . . . one more time before our paths separate."

His words turned her cold. The fire in her veins died out, cooling like melted wax.

"If you love me—" she began, but he covered her mouth with his, quieting her. When she sighed in silent protest, her still-erect nipples encountered the tangle of hair on his chest and were teased into all-consuming demand.

His hand, fingers spread, followed the flatness of her diaphragm, covered the slight swell of her belly and hovered enticingly above the sensitive triangle between her legs. She was pulsating with eagerness. Her hips thrust her most secret self into his hand. His tongue made a wet and stinging trail down the center of her body from breast to navel and beyond. She felt his hands slide down the silken insides of her thighs and press her legs farther apart.

In the night's blackness and the drumming rain, feeling was the totality of experience. She ached for Dave. She lifted her loins in silent supplication. His hands slid beneath her to clasp the yielding flesh of her buttocks. When he saluted the secret core of her, her cry of gratification was warm and human against the tumult of the storm. She felt that she was melting with pleasure. Yet she wanted more. She wanted him to fill her with his maleness.

"Dave, please, please!"

"Are you pleased?"

"You know I am!" Her hands clasped his shoulders, urging him to make them one, and when he did so, when she felt the silken thrust of his manhood, she was shaken by exultation even while tears sprang to her eyes at the thought of all the nights they had lain apart when they might have made love. His deep, hungry thrusts took her quickly over the brink to floating delirium. Dave felt her response and followed with a shout of triumph.

They emerged together, floating in each other's arms, out of a formless tunnel.

At last he drew a deep breath. "I can't get enough of you, Rowen. You're all I ever wanted in a woman." After a moment he added, "Money aside."

"You can't have me without it," she tried to say lightly, aware that with morning their problems would come crowding back.

Wrapped in Dave's arms, she fell asleep, filled with gratitude for life.

Some time later she was awakened by his restlessness.

"Are you warm enough?" she whispered.

His thumb rasped the tip of her breast, and she gasped. She felt him laugh. "I'll show you how warm I am!" He thrust the proof between her legs. Drowsily, deeply stirred, she welcomed him into her again, conscious of fierce exultation. They had made love with ferocity and with tenderness. If they could love like this, how could Dave live without her?

10

~coooooooooo~

They arrived back in New York on Sunday afternoon, parked in front of the apartment building and unloaded. Dave went with Rowen when she returned her car to the garage. He stood by while she instructed the garage attendant to wash it and change the oil.

"Pretty nice," he said when they left. "You lift a finger and it's done."

"Surely you don't think I should do it myself?"

Dave's eyes slid away from hers. "No. . . . It's just . . . . so easy."

"That's the *only* difference between us, Dave," Rowen pressed, glad of a chance to discuss their problem. "Money lets me to do what I want to do. I can learn how to buy rare books instead of clerking in a bookshop. Darling, it could be easy for us both! You could be drawing cartoons instead of advertising artwork."

"I plan to do that anyway." Dave's voice was so gruff that she dropped the subject.

They dined at a neighborhood restaurant before going home. By the time they finished eating, Rowen's tiredness made itself felt. They'd had a long drive that day, and not much sleep the night before. She covered a yawn.

"Looks like you're ready for bed," Dave suggested.

A smile twinkled in her eyes, and she cocked her head at him. "Ready if you are."

Again Dave's eyes slid away. "Not tonight. I want to unpack and go through my mail. There should be some checks. . . ." His voice faded as he realized how laughable the amounts would appear to a person with her kind of money. Then he couldn't bear to see the way her face fell. He picked up the bill and stalked to the cash register.

They walked home in silence. Dave attempted to compose an explanation she could accept.

At her door he said, "The trip didn't show you what I thought it would, Rowen, but I know I'm right." The thought of what his brothers and brothers-in-law would say about his running after a rich woman made him cringe. "I can't swallow my pride. I'm sorry."

Rowen bit her lip and turned to unlock her door.

"Good night, Dave." She held back her tears until she was alone. She, too, had pride.

She didn't get her mail from her next-door neighbor until the following morning. She carried it to work in her briefcase, but she and Horace had so much to talk about that she didn't open her letters until nearly closing time. At the bottom of the stack she came upon an official letter that stunned her.

She made straight for Dave's apartment as soon as she got home and waved the letter in his face.

"Do they mean this? Can they decide to make a building co-op, just like that? Did you get one, too?"

"I did, and they can. I understand the notice arrived the day we left. Some of the tenants held a meeting and talked to a lawyer. I take it you just got home. Want a glass of wine?"

"Please." Rowen sat on the lumpy couch, absently petting

one of the kittens, and looked around the room. It seemed a long time since she'd been there. Nothing had changed except the work on Dave's drawing board.

"What will you do?" she asked when she saw him bringing two glasses and the jug.

"Lose my rent-controlled apartment—that's what I'll do!"

"Yes, but . . ."

"Sorry. I don't mean to snap your head off, but I'm mad. I've been here six years. Now this!" He raised his glass and took a long swallow of burgundy.

"You'll find another place," Rowen said, trying to ignore a slash of pain. They would have to separate if they lost their apartments. That didn't seem to bother him a bit.

"Oh, will I?" He gave her a fierce look. "I suppose I can just walk out and take my choice. This will mean moving to Queens or some other remote place!" He tossed off his wine and poured more. "I didn't leave Missouri to go and live in Queens!"

"Are you hungry?" Rowen asked. "I don't want to drink any more on an empty stomach."

"No, thanks. I had a late lunch."

He didn't offer her anything to munch on, or suggest they go out later, so she said good-bye.

On the way downstairs she wondered if she should have told him her idea for solving the problem, but she decided that she had better talk to her trustees first.

Next evening she bought a good wine on the way home and stopped at the delicatessen. She telephoned Dave from her apartment, happy about what she had to tell him.

"Dave, would you like to come down for a drink? I have something to talk about."

"What?"

"I need your advice. Of course, if you're busy . . ."

"Give me ten minutes."

Happily she set out cheese and crackers, cut celery sticks and opened the wine.

In less than ten minutes Dave appeared, freshly shaven but

lacking his usual glow of good humor. Rowen resisted touching his cheek. Then she wondered why she should resist.

She poured the wine and raised her glass. "Here's to my idea."

He took a swallow. She sat smiling while his blue eyes ran over her, checking to see if she was all right, all together, as though it had been weeks since he'd seen her. She felt warmed by his regard.

"Which is?" he prompted.

A faint doubt crept into her mind. She had been so pleased with her plan. Now, face-to-face with him, she wasn't so sure, but she drew a deep breath and spoke confidently. "Why don't I buy both apartments?"

Carefully, without looking at her, he set down his wine glass.

"You can go on using your as a studio and pay me rent, if you insist," she said nervously.

His eyes narrowed. He gazed around the room as though he'd never seen it before. Slowly a red tide suffused his neck and cheeks. His eyes were bright with anger. Rowen shrank back against the couch. Dave glared at her, his look anything but loving.

"Everything's easy for you, isn't it, Miss Moneybags? You won't buy one apartment, you'll buy two!"

"The money has to be invested somewhere, so why not here? Or a newer apartment." She rushed on. "Bigger, if you want. We could look around! Dave, let me help. Please!"

"And what do you get out of it? Me?"

Rowen failed to suppress a nervous giggle. "You sound like a threatened virgin," she explained, attempting to laugh it off.

"And what you want is a handy stud!" He jumped to his feet, drawing his pride around him like a cape.

"No, I don't! Well, of course, I want to be with you, but this idea . . . I just wanted to help, Dave. We could get a loft, if you'd rather. . . ."

He stalked to the door, turned back and jabbed a finger at her. "You're devious, Rowen Hill! Not an outright liar, but devious. You came around looking cold and skinny and hungry until you had me falling all over myself wanting to take care of you and protect you from the big, bad city. The next thing I know you've got me laid out on a slab, trussed up like a turkey."

"That's because you *are* a turkey!" she shouted.

They stood glaring at each other while their ridiculous insults echoed in their ears. Dave brushed back a lock of hair from his forehead and gave a sour laugh.

"Maybe I am. Thanks, Rowen, but no thanks." He closed the door behind him and was gone.

Rowen wrapped up the cheese. She refilled her glass and drank the wine thoughtfully. She and Dave had had so many final scenes that she didn't panic as she once would have. But if they had to move, it would really be the end. She could hardly chase him around town every time he changed apartments.

For two weeks Dave doggedly looked for an apartment. He was sure the task was hopeless. Furthermore, he didn't want to succeed. He wanted to stay where he was, in his own bare, excellently lighted studio, with Rowen downstairs where he knew what she was up to.

Despite the ferment, he drew a series of really funny cartoons. His editor not only laughed, but bought them. Evenings he sat at his drawing board, doodling and thinking, sketching the now gangly kittens or grimacing into a mirror, finding better ways to show emotions with a few lines—disgust, boredom, befuddlement. He worked out a caricature of Rowen, hardly aware of what he was doing, except that she was always in his mind's eye.

He became absorbed in making an elaborate cartoon of her in an elegant room surrounded by a passel of squawling brats, each brat with its own white-uniformed nursemaid. His quirky humor asserted itself, and he filled the empty spaces with Himalayan cats and kittens. He added Vicky and a pair of Russian wolfhounds.

When he finished, he tacked up the drawing and studied it. He realized that he had created a household he himself wanted.

Exaggerated, of course, but not wildly. Rowen's babies *would* have nursemaids—maybe not one each. No kids underfoot for her. Just dogs. And cats.

Then he remembered what he had said about kids underfoot. Cautiously he confronted his feelings.

"I said I wanted a rich wife," he admitted aloud. "And fate sent one along."

God knows, I love her, he went on thinking. So what's keeping me from blessing my lucky stars? Why do I think there's something shameful about marrying a woman I love? Her circumstances be damned!

He wondered how it would feel not to be responsible for even the most basic bills—the rent, the electricity. He tried to imagine whether he would feel pleasantly light or simply adrift without the spur of necessity.

What would his relatives say? His friends? Would they think he'd married for money? He hadn't thought he cared about other people's opinions. That just went to show how a person didn't know himself until the time came. In Missouri no one had guessed Rowen was wealthy. She hadn't flaunted it; she never did. That brought up a point. Who would know?

If she *had* flaunted it, he wouldn't have fallen for her!

He threw down his pencil in disgust and went to the kitchen to open a beer. He was angry because she had deceived him. So what? Had it harmed him? Yes. If he'd known she was rich, he wouldn't have felt concerned for her. He wouldn't have let her disrupt his life.

For the first time he wondered why she had deceived him. What had she expected to gain?

Was he so handsome that she was overwhelmed? He wandered into the bathroom and peered into the mirror. The same ordinary face, needing a shave, peered back at him. Besides, most men would have been bowled over by a rich woman; she just happened to have picked the oddball.

Maybe she hadn't wanted to bowl him over. She certainly hadn't chased him. His smile twisted when he recalled how he and Clancy had hunted her down. No, she hadn't chased him.

She had let him pursue her. Then they had looked in each other's eyes and *kaboom!* they were walking around a foot off the ground. Dave shook his head, bemused by the power of sexual attraction.

Why had she deceived him? What had she expected to gain? The questions kept repeating themselves—while he cooked peppers and eggs for dinner, while he walked Clancy, while he watched the news. Finally he knew he had to ask her.

He also had to find a new apartment. A halfhearted meeting with the building manager told him what he already suspected: Even if he had a down payment, he couldn't obtain a mortgage without a regular job.

He decided to catch Rowen off guard. Three evenings in a row he left his door open, listening for her, but she didn't come straight home from work. Evidently she was eating dinner first, dining with that rip-off artist of a lawyer or another of his ilk. Dave's jaw jutted. That was how people would think about him, if he took up with her again.

He met her outside the building by chance. He had been out in the chilly rain looking at two impossibly expensive apartments, had bought a hamburger to go and tramped home. He was approaching the door when Vicky sprang out of a taxi, followed by Rowen. He felt, as always, the deep thrill that came over him whenever he saw her unexpectedly. His eyes devoured the way she moved, the way her dress hugged her derriere. Possessively he eyed her shapely calves, her impossibly slim ankles. Raindrops sparkled on her dark hair as though she were a princess wearing diamonds.

But when she paid the driver and turned around, the illusion shattered. Her face was pale and she was shivering.

"Rowen . . ." He unlocked the street door and held it open. "Oh, hi!"

By the harsh light of the hall he saw lines of strain etched around her mouth. The sparkle was missing from her brown eyes. They were tired and darkly shadowed. Nor did she greet him with her usual enthusiasm. Her lack of interest made him uneasy.

He noticed the thin jacket she was wearing and concern for her overrode his foolish feeling of pique. He couldn't resist trying to talk some sense into her as he followed her and the dog upstairs.

"You shouldn't be wearing that thin dress on a day like this! Don't you listen to the weather report before you go out? You're looking like the little match girl again—summer version."

"Don't scold. I couldn't find the raincoat I keep at the shop. I didn't realize the weather had turned so cold." She shivered.

As soon as they reached her landing, he put his arm around her, pulling her against him. While she fumbled for her keys, he rubbed her back vigorously, hoping to warm her.

"How many times have I told you?" he growled. "When you live in a building without a doorman, you should have your keys in your hand the moment you walk up to your door. If you're going to live in the city, you've got to be streetwise."

"I know, but I saw you standing there."

He looked at his watch. "How come you're so late?"

She opened the door. Unasked he followed her inside.

"Horace is in the hospital—"

"I'm sorry!" He helped her peel off her wet jacket. "Tell me about it, but go put on some dry clothes first. I'll pour you a glass of wine. Or sherry. Or would you rather have hot coffee?"

"Wine, I think. Maybe it will give me some pep." Vicky danced about the kitchen, anticipating her dinner. The Himalayan cats wove sinuously about Rowen's legs. "Would you mind feeding the animals?" She threw him an apologetic smile and disappeared into her bedroom.

"Have a hot shower," Dave called after her. "I'll wait."

He was opening cans of cat food when he heard the water running. He wondered if she'd eaten anything since lunch. He looked into the refrigerator to see if there was something he could heat up. Nothing. He found frozen dinners in the freezer, but he was hungry, too, and they didn't appeal to him. He looked for crackers to go with the wine. Again nothing.

He took his hamburger out of the bag and cut it in four

pieces. Not classy, but warm food. Rowen had looked like she needed it. After she relaxed and drank some wine he would take her out to eat or get something from the deli.

He carried the French fries that accompanied the hamburger into the living room, sank into one of her comfortable chairs and munched while he waited. His gaze wandered around the room. He basked in its rich comfort and observed the thick foliage of Rowen's plants. She sure had a green thumb. . . .

It hit him that he was happier than he'd been since his return from Missouri. Darn it, he enjoyed looking after her! Cherishing her. It felt right. Where was this guy Stewart? Why wasn't he on the scene if he was so crazy about her?

Eating soggy French fries and drinking expensive wine, Dave realized that he still felt protective. And possessive! But Rowen needed protecting! Having money didn't exempt her from the disasters of life, or the disappointments.

Horace in the hospital. How much of that responsibility had fallen on her? Dave didn't know whether the old man had family in town or not. Even if he did, probably none of them were as close to him as Rowen. Dave had gathered that he treated Rowen as much like a granddaughter as a partner.

Dave heard a drawer close in the bedroom and called to her. "Will you be much longer? I've got some cheese upstairs. . . ."

"Don't bother." She came into the living room. "There should be crackers. . . ." She looked vaguely toward the kitchen.

"There aren't." His breath seemed to choke him. She looked warm and rosy from her shower. She was wearing a long-sleeved cotton dress in glowing colors. He was surprised anew by how beautiful and desirable she was. That seemed to happen each time he saw her. Had he really been so crass as to tell her that men wanted her only for her money?

Looked at with the eyes of love, she was as beautiful as ever, but there was sadness in her dull glance and a tired droop to her sweet mouth.

He wanted to grab her and hold her. He wanted to tell her that he was there to share her troubles, that nothing was so bad when people faced it together, but he had forfeited the right. Instead of being around for support, he had backed away.

"Sit down and eat this while it's warm, and bring me up to date," he said gruffly. He indicated the plate with its pieces of hamburger. He filled her glass with red wine. The vivid color promised cheer and prosperity. Outside a gust of windblown rain splashed the windows.

Rowen looked at his offering and summoned a faint smile. She picked up a piece and nibbled.

Dave swallowed the remains of his share in two bites and took up his glass. "Tell me what's been going on."

Rowen sighed. "Horace had a heart attack. The first I knew was when the hospital called me at the shop. It happened in the evening, while he was home. It's not his first. He was able to call an ambulance."

"When was this?"

She frowned, rubbing one slim hand across her brow. "Three days ago, I think. Yes, Monday. I've been so worried. But he's going to be all right." She smiled and then sighed. "He'll be in the hospital awhile. That's why I'm so tired. I've been spending every evening there."

"And running the shop alone all day?"

"Yes."

"And not eating, I suppose. Rowen, you'll end up in the hospital along with Horace. Can't you hire a clerk?"

"I did. He's starting tomorrow. It's not waiting on customers that's hard. It's making the decisions. Wondering if Horace would approve."

"From the sound of things, it may soon be your shop anyway."

"I hope not." Her eyes turned even sadder.

Dave reached across the table for her hand. "I'm sorry. That was a stupid thing to say."

"It's true. I just hope I know enough."

"I wondered where you've been every evening. I wanted to talk to you."

"About our apartments?" She looked quickly up at him,

hope in her dark eyes. He hated to disappoint her, but he had no choice.

"No. I'm sorry. It was nothing more than curiosity. I wanted to ask you one question."

She raised her delicate brows.

"Why didn't you want me to know you were rich?"

She shrugged.

"That very first evening you pretended you were house-sitting," he pressed. "Why?"

"I *was* house-sitting!"

Dave leaned forward, his eyes on her face. "Yes. You were also working in a used-book store—"

"*Rare* books!"

"All right, *rare* books, but you know what I mean. Darn it, Rowen!" Her evasiveness was making him lose his temper, and he sat back in his chair. "What did you expect to gain?"

Her eyes followed one of the cats as it strolled across the room and leapt onto the couch. She sighed. "It wasn't fair of me; I realize that now. But I didn't know what you were like. I'd built a shell around myself." She raised her eyes. "Do you want to hear my whole life story?"

"Isn't it about time?"

"Maybe. It's just that talking about it doesn't seem to help. I still feel ashamed for being such a fool."

"You may have been innocent, but you weren't a fool!"

"It amounts to the same thing. I was dumb! You see, I was so happy to get married. I thought the sun rose and set on Joe—as they say. Marriage was going to be everything I'd always wanted. I never felt I had any family. All the time I was growing up my grandparents kept telling me how old they were, as if they might die any moment. They wanted to prepare me. Instead, it made me totally insecure, like it might happen without warning—the way my parents died. I had friends at school, of course, but they all scattered after we graduated. I'm not an outgoing person. . . . At least, I try to be, but . . ." She shrugged. "Anyway . . . I guess Joe liked me well enough. He liked women, period. I happened to be a woman with money, so he married me. He was a filmmaker. Not a very good one, but I supported his career. He made a couple of documentaries that weren't bad, actually, but then . . ." She looked bewildered. "He changed. He was always something of an exhibitionist, I suppose, but he met a couple of crazy women. He began making porn films first, and then he began living them. I found out one night when I went to his studio. It was an old barn out in the country. He was supposed to be processing film. . . ."

Dave made a disgusted sound. "How did that make you a fool?" he asked when she was silent.

"I should have sensed how crazy he was, don't you think? I shouldn't have been in such a hurry to marry him. I felt used. And stupid. Why didn't I see what he was?" She raised tortured eyes to Dave's.

"Because you were in love with him."

"No. In love with the idea of belonging with someone. So when I met you . . ." She bit her lip and stared at the rain-drenched window.

"Go on."

"It's hard to explain. . . . When I met you, I felt I was getting even somehow by keeping my real self a secret. I couldn't get involved if you didn't know the real me. I even decided not to see you again. But you insisted. So I figured I'd see what would happen if I wasn't rich. If you'd like me for myself. You did, didn't you?"

"Oh, Rowen." Dave moved to the couch and put his arm around her.

"After I knew you better . . ." She picked up his hand and ran a finger across his knuckles. "After we fell in love . . . I did tell you, but it didn't occur to you that I had so much. I keep telling myself there's a man somewhere with courage enough to love me *and* my money."

"Well, sure." Dave tried to ignore the flame of jealousy that leapt at her words. "You just have to find a good man with money of his own."

"You think that's easy?" Her smile was bitter, making him feel like a heel, though he couldn't figure what he'd done wrong.

"Listen, you may be streetwise, but I know something about wealthy men. They're usually three deep in women willing to cater to their every whim. They're arrogant and selfish and deadly dull. My grandparents may have been old, but they brought me up among real people. My grandfather and his cronies earned their money. If I can't find a man who has character and strength and appreciates me for myself, I'll go it alone." Her eyes flashed.

Dave watched her with ever-new fascination. She could change with bewildering speed from a wistful waif to a spirited feminist to a bewitching, adorable armful, which was the way he saw her at that instant. He reached for her.

Rowen was determined not to react. Either they were friendly acquaintances, or they were lovers. She was tired of Dave's games, tired of being swept to the moon and then dropped sprawling back to earth.

When he reached out to take her in his arms, she stood up and crossed the room to the window.

"It's still raining," she reported, gazing down at the shining reflections on the dark street. She felt Dave come up behind her.

"Rowen . . ." His hands clasped her waist, at first comforting; then, as their warmth communicated itself to her through the material of her dress, she felt herself melting, her bad humor slipping away to be replaced by excitement and wonder.

For what seemed eons he simply stood there, not speaking, his fingers grasping her sides, and let his touch wreak havoc with her stern intentions. She ought to move, be the one to break away. Despite herself, her breath came faster. Her breast rose and fell as desire smoldered and burst into flame.

She felt his lips on her neck. Suddenly the only thought in her mind was to let her body meld into his. His arms surrounded her, crossing beneath her breasts. She felt the urgency of his arousal hard against her buttocks and knew, without surprise, that her greed for Dave was total. She wanted as much of him as she could get, by whatever means.

He was honorable and virtuous. She was willing to tell fibs and be devious, and use her money to buy him, if it would work. If he wanted to make new rules every few days, she'd go along. She spun around in his arms, laughter springing to her lips.

"You can't keep away from me, Dave Archer! Admit it."

Dave's mouth covered hers in passionate agreement. "I can't!" he groaned. "It's true! I can't."

Rowen let herself drift upon the kiss, aware only of the strength of Dave's arms, the glorious masculine scent of him, the rasp of his breathing—or was it hers?

The silence of the room was shattered by the raucous buzz of the downstairs door.

Rowen came to her senses with a start.

"Leave it," Dave muttered. "Some idiot's forgotten his key." He would have recaptured her lips, but she held him off.

"It's Stewart Sawyer," she confessed, her face warm with passion and embarrassment. "I forgot about him! We're going to the hospital, and then he's taking me out to dinner."

11

Dave dropped his hands, astonished that Rowen could do such a thing—forget she had a date, lead him on like that. A surge of anger replaced the passion that had consumed him a moment before. He stared at her in disbelief.

"You forgot! You left me dangling on a twig while you showered and dressed to go out, and then you *forgot?* I don't believe it!"

"I did! I honestly did!" She gazed back at him, her expression troubled. One finger went to her lips. "Everything's been so hectic, and I was so glad to see you. . . ."

"Stop biting your nails!" He couldn't believe she was going to walk out of her apartment with another man when he had been planning . . . He tore his mind from what he'd been planning and let rage take over. "Rowen, you're being devious again! And lying!"

He saw surprise in the look she gave him.

"I believe you're jealous!"

He said a four-letter word, but she looked knowing.

"You were exhausted!" he shouted. "I felt sorry for you. Then, presto! You're ready to go out on the town."

"Is that what you call visiting the hospital?" She disappeared into the bedroom and came back with a tiny, frivolous purse that somehow made him angrier than ever. It was purple, and now that he noticed, it matched her shoes. The supple leather bag with its tiny shoulder strap had probably cost as much as he earned in a day. It was designed to hold nothing more than a comb, key, lipstick and mad money.

Before he could untangle his emotions, Stewart rapped on the door.

"Dave, please stop scowling," Rowen requested and ushered the lawyer in. He was wearing the latest in trench coats over a dark suit. Dave became conscious of his zippered sweatshirt jacket, old jeans and sneakers.

"You remember each other," Rowen said. "You met at Celia's cocktail party."

"You're the comedian," Stewart said.

"Cartoonist," Dave corrected, smiling through his teeth. It would give him a lot of satisfaction to slam his fist against that smooth jawline! Instead, he shook hands. How many men over the centuries had shaken hands with gritted teeth, he wondered.

"Ready?" Stewart asked Rowen.

She indicated that she was.

"See you later," Dave muttered.

He had to climb the stairs and watch the woman he loved—the woman who had claimed to love him—walk in the other direction, with Stewart's arm about her waist.

Dave unlocked his door, feeling low. No Rowen and no studio. And all he'd had for dinner was half a hamburger and some faded French fries. He'd have to go out again. The prospect, which hadn't bothered him at all when he'd expected to take Rowen, now seemed incredibly depressing.

He fed Clancy and the cats and poured himself a large bourbon. Maybe he wouldn't eat; maybe he'd stay there and get drunk. No, he had to finish the layouts he'd promised for the following morning.

He tipped the bourbon into the sink, reached for his trench coat—a much shabbier affair than Stewart's—and plodded out to get another burger.

Back in his apartment, he unwrapped the food to find his appetite gone. He hoped Rowen was eating a square meal. He tried not to imagine her with Stewart, in a candlelit room, at an intimate table where the creep could look into her guileless brown eyes and propose again. Fear touched his stomach. It made the hamburger even more tasteless. He removed the slice of onion. If he hoped to see Rowen later . . . How could he see her later? She might bring Stewart home. She had every right. He himself had refused to make any commitment, and from what she had said, Stewart was all eagerness.

He flung the hamburger down on its wrapper and defiantly made himself a drink, pouring bourbon over ice cubes and adding a few drops of water. There were times in a man's life when bourbon was the only answer. He sat down at the drawing board and picked up his lettering pen.

Two hours of concentrated work later, he gave the last sheet the finishing touches, sat back and stretched. The hamburger had cooled. The ice in his drink had melted, leaving a half-filled glass of brown-tinted water.

He laid the finished work aside, picked up his drink and slouched to the window. Down in the street, puddles smoothly reflected the streetlights, unmarred by falling raindrops. In the bedroom Dave heard the kittens romping. He began thinking about Rowen's husband. What a weirdo he must have been! And what a jerk! Ego gratification—that was all those films could have been. To lose Rowen over something so slimy! The man had been a real bastard to take advantage of someone as defenseless as Rowen. No wonder she was suspicious of men. He hoped her suspicion extended to Stewart!

He smiled. She wouldn't like being termed "defenseless." But that was the impression she created. At least with him. He

175

couldn't seem to stop wanting to defend her, to protect her from all the crazy people who would circle her wealth like vultures. She deserved a decent man.

The idea of Rowen living on her own in New York, running her shop alone, made him uncomfortable. He would certainly keep a protective eye on her until that decent someone came along . . . a man to whom her fortune wouldn't be important, who wouldn't need to think about money himself.

The thought of turning her over to that man made his hackles rise. He tried to picture a paragon worthy of Rowen, someone he could stomach, too.

He sat on the couch, legs apart, forearms on his knees. Clancy rolled soulful brown eyes in his direction.

"Are you looking at me?" he demanded of the dog. "Maybe you're right! Where's she going to find anyone as decent as I am? *I'm the kind of man she needs! Because I sure as hell don't want anyone else to fill the role!*" He set his empty glass aside and coaxed Clancy to come and be petted.

"I've changed my mind, Clancy. She needs me. She's all alone, do you realize? She'd be marrying into a family, not that it's any special deal, but she seemed to like it. It's something I could offer, something she doesn't have."

He held the hound's ears straight out to the sides and gazed into the trusting eyes. "Truth is, Clancy, it's okay to belong to a big family, but I want someone of my own. I want Rowen, and damn what people say. We'll work it out." His laugh was short. "Maybe it won't even be too painful."

Again he tried to imagine what it would be like to be free of any financial burden. "I'll have to suffer all the way to the bank!" He managed a hollow laugh. However they handled the finances, he knew he could count on Rowen's tact. She'd grown up with money; it was no big deal to her.

He looked at his watch. How soon would she come home so he could tell her? He jumped up and strode about the room, the excitement of his decision making his blood race. Suddenly he smacked his forehead. What if that creep Stewart came back upstairs with her? What if . . . ? He couldn't bear to put the thought into words. The very idea made his head spin.

Then he remembered that he still had a key to Rowen's door. He wasn't locked out! An idea of how to take care of Stewart popped into his head. "Yippee!" He did an impromptu war dance.

He ran into his bedroom and dumped out the box that held his cuff links. During the time he'd been so angry at her for being rich, he'd taken her key off his chain and tossed it . . . somewhere. Now, when every minute counted, he couldn't find it. It wasn't in the box. He ran to open the hall door so he could listen for her—them. If they returned before he could get down there, his scheme wouldn't work. Swearing, he scrabbled through the places where odds and ends collected and finally thought of the drawer in the taboret, where he kept his inks and pens.

That was it! He remembered now; he'd been fuming over Rowen's deception one day at the drawing board. He had taken the key off his ring and tossed it in the drawer.

He found it and raced into the bedroom. He jerked open the drawer where he kept the fine cotton pajamas Rowen had given him—because they matched his eyes. He snatched them up . . . slippers . . . robe. . . . Chuckling over the diabolical way he was about to triumph over one preppy lawyer, he ran down the flight and let himself into her apartment.

Twenty minutes later Rowen climbed the stairs, only half listening to Stewart grumbling about buildings without elevators.

"You didn't have to come up," she reminded him.

"Yes, I did, if I'm going to have that nightcap."

"I didn't offer you a nightcap," she said as they reached her landing.

"I'm hoping you will." Before he could take her key, she unlocked the door herself. He slipped his arm about her waist.

"Very well, since you've made such a big effort to climb the stairs." Rebelliously, she felt that Stewart's presence might make her less lonely for Dave.

She stepped ahead of Stewart into her softly lighted apartment. The glow from the elegant lamps fell on the rich colors of the room.

And on Dave.

He was seated in one of the comfortable chairs, wearing pajamas, a robe and slippers, with Vicky at his feet. He looked up from his book, presenting the perfect picture of the relaxed man of the house.

Rowen stopped so suddenly that Stewart bumped into her. She heard his sharp intake of breath.

Dave laid aside his book and stood up. He looked warmly welcoming, and Rowen suppressed a sigh. If only it were true! With what pleasure she would fling herself on his chest.

"How did you find Horace?" he inquired into the silence. He came forward, nodded to Stewart and benignly kissed Rowen's cheek, for all the world like a husband welcoming his wife and the family lawyer. It was all Rowen could do not to laugh when she turned and saw Stewart's bulging eyes. She kept her countenance, but questions roiled in her mind. What kind of joke was Dave playing?

"Horace is recovering fast," she answered with poise. "He wants to go home. Let me take your coat, Stewart."

She hung it in the hall closet and gathered her wits. How dare Dave put on such a phony show? If she'd been serious about Stewart, it would have been unforgivable. Actually, she was vastly relieved not to be alone with him. But Dave had no way of knowing that!

"Stewart and I are having a nightcap," she said coldly. "Are you joining us?"

The silver tray on the Swedish modern sideboard held a wide assortment of liqueurs. Stewart chose the currently chic one; Dave chose brandy. Dutch courage? Rowen wondered. Perhaps he wasn't at ease, despite the way he had been lounging in her chair. She sipped her usual *creme de menthe* and tried to steer the conversation along civilized lines. Stewart was no doubt burning to complain that she'd misled him, and she herself was fuming. Half her mind was on what she was going to say to Dave the minute Stewart left. If she had to keep up with this polite pretense for long, steam would come out of her ears.

Luckily, Stewart tossed off his tiny glassful and got up to leave. Rowen fetched his coat.

"You have some explaining to do," he informed her at the door. "Although I guess it's pretty clear what's going on."

"It's not clear at all!" Rowen snapped, holding her temper by a thread. "Call me at the shop tomorrow."

"Good night!" Dave called genially from the living room.

She closed the door after Stewart and stood fighting for self-control. By now she was in such a state, with so many accusations to hurl at Dave, that she didn't know where to begin.

She walked into the living room, her face stony. Dave came around the coffee table to meet her.

"All right, why did you do it?" she cried.

"I wanted to protect you." Dave's halfhearted grin fanned the flames of her anger. He looked like a large puppy, expecting to be punished, yet hoping to be forgiven.

Then his assurance returned, and he laughed. "You should have seen his face! I couldn't have gotten more pleasure out of knocking him down!" At last he accepted Rowen's expression, and the laughter went out of his eyes. "You're mad."

"Of course I'm mad! What right do you have to come in here, creating this phony scene—the big, loving and protective male? That's not what you are! What you are is a dog in the manger!"

Dave was silent, stung by the knowledge that her words contained a grain of truth. "Rowen, I've been thinking. . . ." His mind had been whirling furiously in the last few hours. He felt drained.

"You're always thinking!" She picked up her practically untouched glass and Stewart's empty one and carried them to the kitchen. Dave followed.

"Rowen, we need to talk."

"Maybe you do!" She turned on him fiercely. "I don't! I'm going to bed. Alone. So will you please get out?" She reached for the doorknob.

Dave's emotional state needed an outlet. He felt as though he had gone through a tornado in the couple of hours since he'd last seen her. First he'd made the decision to marry her; then for twenty minutes he'd sat in her living room, waiting. His lively imagination had pictured a quarrel—a fight—where he knocked Stewart down. Or worse, Stewart knocked him down. Worst of all, Rowen threw him out and kept Stewart. He was too late. He had lost her.

"Rowen, you have to listen to me!" Glorying in his strength, he snatched her into his arms. She began to struggle, but he carried her into the bedroom.

"Stop it!" she shrieked. "Put me down!"

Instead of depositing her on the bed, as he'd intended, he held on to her, subduing her wriggling body while he tried to argue. "Please! It'll only take—"

"I mean it!" she cried, pounding his chest with her fists. "I hate you! Put me down!"

The excitement of finally holding her made him lose his head. He was doing his best to kiss her when he heard a snarl. Too late he recognized the danger. Sharp teeth and strong jaws closed on his leg. This time he wasn't wearing boots.

He loosed Rowen with an oath, using all his willpower to stay calm and still. Vicky had a good, firm hold on the fleshy curve of his calf. Her lips curled back viciously. Her little pink-rimmed eyes stared up at him as though to say, "I haven't clamped down yet, but if you dare move . . ."

"Vicky!" Rowen dropped down beside the dog, reaching to pull the canine jaws apart.

"Don't do it!" Dave ordered, but she shook her head at him.

"Vicky!" she coaxed. "It's Dave! Stop it! We were playing."

Reluctantly, it seemed to Dave, Vicky let go and backed away.

"Oh, thank heavens! That's a good dog!" Rowen sagged back against the bed.

Dave sank onto it and pulled up his pajama leg to inspect the damage. He was embarrassed to find his hands shaking. Rowen, on eye level with his leg, inspected the red mark.

"Oh, bless her heart, she didn't even break the skin!" She laughed breathlessly. Vicky sat in the doorway, panting gently. "Bad dog! Dave's your friend!" Rowen put a hand over her mouth, but her eyes were sparkling.

"You're laughing!" Dave accused her. He jumped to his feet and stormed out of the bedroom, angrier than he'd ever been in his life. "When I think of the times I've fed her, and walked her! She's the most ungrateful bitch I've ever known! You don't need me!" He waved a finger under Rowen's nose. "Between your money and your dog, you don't need me for anything!"

Rowen's face sobered. "How can you blame Vicky for protecting me?"

"How can Vicky be so dumb?" Dave didn't try to mask his hurt feelings. "I've been like a father to that dog. Okay, I got the message loud and clear." He reached for the doorknob.

"Where are you going?" Rowen cried.

"Home!"

"I thought you wanted to talk!"

"Talk to Vicky!"

"You know what your trouble is?" she spat after him. "You have no sense of humor!" Behind his back the door was slammed and locked.

Upstairs he made himself a drink and turned on the television. He didn't know when his feelings had been so ruffled. So much for what he'd wanted to tell her.

The black-and-white screen was showing the replay of a baseball game, a backdrop for his brooding thoughts.

It took him half an hour to cool down. His mind flashed him a picture of how he must have looked with Vicky clamped to his leg and suddenly he saw that it *was* amusing. If a cartoonist couldn't laugh at himself, he was in a bad way. No wonder Rowen had giggled. Vicky had certainly shattered the romantic scene he had planned.

So he had no sense of humor! He managed a feeble smile

and looked at his watch. Too late to go back and apologize now. She was exhausted. He'd been a fool to try to talk to her at the end of such a long day. Tomorrow morning, when she was rested. . . . He couldn't wait longer than that. He'd tell her that he was the right man for her despite her money, and then he'd walk her to work.

He fell asleep, grinning at the memory of Stewart's face when he'd walked in. On the other hand, being bitten by Vicky—even if she didn't break the skin—was not funny, no matter what Rowen thought.

Perhaps because of the emotional storm, Dave overslept, and for once the cats didn't wake him, demanding food. By the time he showered and dressed and knocked on Rowen's door, she had gone. He took Clancy out for his morning stroll and tried to think sanely. What he wanted to do was charge madly into the bookshop and declare his intention of marrying her, but he soon saw that telling her impulsively that he'd had a change of mind might not work. Better to make an occasion of it, maybe even set it up ahead of time, what with Horace in the hospital. Tonight wasn't good, not when she had to open the shop on Saturday. Tomorrow night would be perfect. If things went right, they could spend all day Sunday in bed.

He hurried upstairs and telephoned the bookshop. He decided not to mention the night before.

"Hi, love," he said when she picked up the phone. "It's me, Dave. Rowen . . . would you have dinner with me? Tonight?" When it came down to it, he couldn't wait. "We could go to the hospital before . . . or afterward, whichever suits you best."

"No . . ."

"No, which?"

"No, I won't have dinner with you, Dave." Her voice was cooler than he'd ever heard it.

"Tomorrow night, then! I have to see you." He sounded desperate, even to himself.

"No, thank you, Dave. I'm sure you don't have anything to tell me that you haven't already said."

"But I do!"

"I have too much on my mind with Horace and the shop. Maybe later, when he's better. I've got a customer, Dave. I have to hang up."

He dropped the phone and ran his hands through his hair. What now? Something had to be done. He wouldn't be fit for anything until this business was settled. If she said no, he might *never* be fit for anything.

How could he get her attention long enough to say his piece? He turned over various wild possibilities, such as writing it on a continuous roll of paper and lowering it from his window to hers, but the wind would grab it, or she might simply turn her back. He thought of sending Clancy to her door with a portable tape player playing his message, but that was silly, too. She might turn off the tape.

He still had the key to her apartment. Maybe he should meet her in bed. Something told him that would go over like a lead balloon. No, he had to think of something really terrific . . . something funny.

As he tried to think, he realized that he had never shown Rowen any of the cartoons he'd done of her. Nor had he ever given her a drawing. So much else had been going on. . . . The least he should have done was give her a drawing of Vicky. He would go through his stacks of sketches.

He had a couple of empty frames with glass in them. The long, narrow one would work best. He decided to draw four poses in a row and put the finished product in her apartment. She'd see it when she came home and know he had forgiven Vicky. Maybe she would forgive him and listen to his proposal. As he hunted for the sketches he'd made of Vicky, he found himself whistling.

Near the top of the second pile, he came across the cartoon he'd done of Rowen two days before, the one where she was surrounded by babies, nursemaids, cats and dogs. Now *there* was humor! It put him in a good mood just to look at the assortment of kittens. And the clones of babies and nursemaids, he chuckled.

Suddenly he laughed aloud. *This* was the way to get his message to Rowen! All he had to do was put himself in the picture. She'd get the point.

He pulled out a fresh sheet of drawing paper and flung himself into his chair and began roughing in the figures. He replaced the Russian wolfhounds with Clancy. The question was where to put himself. On one knee, popping the question? A little late for that with babies all over the place. Then in his mind the scene perfected itself. Half the room would have the elegant background of her apartment; the other half would be bare like his studio, with him at his drawing table. Cats and kittens and babies and nursemaids would be overrunning both sides. If that didn't get his point across, nothing would.

He finished the drawing shortly before five o'clock and quickly framed the pen-and-ink sketches of Vicky. The cartoon was too big to frame. At the last minute he was afraid she wouldn't get the message. He wrote, "Marry me!" in red felt marker on a fifteen-inch strip of paper and rolled it up.

In Rowen's apartment he propped Vicky's pictures on the kitchen counter. He fastened the cartoon across the front of the refrigerator with four magnets. Inside the refrigerator he hung the mannequin's hand holding the rolled-up banner. When Rowen opened the door to get cat food, it would unroll. He tried it several times to make sure.

"If that doesn't get my message across, nothing will," he told her curious cats before he locked her door and went back upstairs.

Now what to do while he waited? Drinking was out. He didn't want to be drunk when she came up the stairs laughing her silvery laugh. He had never thought of describing it that way before, but it *was* silvery. He couldn't just pace the floor, but what else was there? What if she didn't come home? He had heard her tell Stewart to call her at the shop. What if Stewart took her to *his* place? She'd have Vicky along, but Stewart wouldn't object. Or Stewart might come with her to bring Vicky home. He would see Dave's offerings . . . and Rowen would laugh carelessly. Dave ran a shaking hand through his hair and groaned.

He poured himself a small drink after all and turned on the television. Women spent lots of time waiting for men. He wondered how they stood it. He remembered his sisters waiting for telephone calls when he was growing up. They had wandered irritably about the house, just as he was doing.

An hour later he was pretending to watch a news program when a knock came on his door. He jumped off the bed and strode out to open it, holding his breath as he hoped that it would be Rowen.

It was. She was laughing. She had never looked more beautiful. She had the big cartoon in her hand.

"Dave, it's darling! I love it! Is it supposed to mean . . . ?" She looked at him doubtfully.

"Come in here," he said, taking her by the wrist.

She stepped inside, and he closed the door and threw his arms around her. He buried his face in her hair, inhaling deeply.

"Didn't you look in the icebox?" he murmured, kissing her ear.

"What's in there? I saw this and . . . Oh, Dave, how could I stay angry?" She began to laugh. "What are all these babies? Are they supposed to be ours?"

"Only if you marry me." Dave held her away and looked into her face.

Her brown eyes began to sparkle. "Do you mean it?" she whispered. "Oh, Dave!"

The electrical current that hadn't been flowing too well between them lately suddenly came to life, as if someone had turned up the voltage. Rowen threw her arms about his neck.

"Of course, I will!"

Dave had taken time earlier to make one important purchase. A bottle of chilled champagne was waiting hopefully in the refrigerator. He carried Rowen into his studio and seated her on the lumpy couch. He brought out his two stemmed glasses and popped the cork.

"To us."

Gazing into each other's eyes, they drank.

"You kept saying you wanted to talk to me," Rowen said happily. "Why didn't you tell me what it was about? When did you make up your mind?

"Yesterday. I did a lot of thinking. The only man I could stand the thought of your marrying was me. Rowen—" He reached for her hand, his blue eyes unwavering. "I don't know how this money thing will work out, or even where we'll end up living. It's bound to be traumatic, but I'm willing to try. I love you too much to give you up. That's all I have to offer. Love and loyalty and a lot of in-laws! Will that be enough?"

"Absolutely!" Rowen said, beginning to kiss his smiling lips. "Dave, can we get married in Missouri? Will all your family come to the wedding?"

"Try keeping them away!" He knew then that he truly *did* have something to offer, something much more valuable than two million dollars.

Rebecca had set herself on course for loneliness and despair. It took a plane crash and a struggle to survive in the wilds of the Canadian Northwest Territories to make her change – and to let her fall in love with the only other survivor, handsome Guy McLaren.

Arctic Rose is her story – and you can read it from the 14th February for just £2.25.

The story continues with Rebecca's sister, Tamara, available soon.

COMING NEXT MONTH

STARLIGHT
Penelope Wisdom

Could Trevor ever trust Stephen again? She'd forced
herself to think of him as an evil dragon — to protect
herself from him. Could Stephen convince her that
he was really her knight in shining armor?

YEAR OF THE POET
Ann Hurley

After Joyce had spent months chasing the Irish poet
Neill all over town, her research was at a standstill,
but her feelings had accelerated with the speed of a
frenzied wind. Joyce would never be the same after
this year of the poet.

A BIRD IN THE HAND
Dixie Browning

Anny knew she could help heal Tyrus — she was
accustomed to rehabilitating the wildest of wild
creatures — only she hadn't meant to lose her heart
in the process!

Silhouette Desire

COMING NEXT MONTH

BEYOND LOVE
Ann Major

The day spilled into years and Morgan came after her. Could they pick up the pieces, or would Dinah's insecurity destroy a passion that went beyond love?

THE TENDER STRANGER
Diane Palmer

Eric said he needed freedom, yet he'd married her. He said he hated women, yet he tenderly conquered her heart. Was it possible to meet a soldier of fortune on the battleground of passion and win the war of love?

MOON MADNESS
Freda Vasilos

Jason was still the only man for Sophie, and she was determined to recapture that time of passion — the enchantment of moon madness.

Silhouette Desire

Silhouette Desire Romances

TAKE 4
THRILLING SILHOUETTE
DESIRE ROMANCES
ABSOLUTELY FREE

Experience all the excitement, passion and pure joy of love. Discover fascinating stories brought to you by Silhouette's top selling authors. At last an opportunity for you to become a regular reader of Silhouette Desire. You can enjoy 6 superb new titles every month from Silhouette Reader Service, with a whole range of special benefits, a free monthly Newsletter packed with recipes, competitions and exclusive book offers. Plus information on the top Silhouette authors, a monthly guide to the stars and extra bargain offers.

An Introductory FREE GIFT for YOU.
Turn over the page for details.

As a special introduction we will send you **FOUR**
specially selected Silhouette Desire romances
— yours to keep FREE — when you complete
and return this coupon to us.

At the same time, because we believe that you will be so thrilled
with these novels, we will reserve a subscription to Silhouette
Reader Service for you. Every month you will receive 6 of the very
latest novels by leading romantic fiction authors, delivered direct to
your door.

Postage and packing is always completely
free. There is no obligation or commitment —
you can cancel your subscription at any time.

It's so easy. Send no money now. Simply fill in and post
the coupon today to:-
SILHOUETTE READER SERVICE, FREEPOST,
P.O. Box 236 Croydon, SURREY CR9 9EL

Please note: READERS IN SOUTH AFRICA to write to:-
Silhouette, Postbag X3010 Randburg 2125 S. Africa

- -

FREE BOOKS CERTIFICATE

To: Silhouette Reader Service, FREEPOST, PO Box 236,
Croydon, Surrey CR9 9EL

Please send me, Free and without obligation, four specially selected Silhouette Desire Romances and reserve a
Reader Service Subscription for me. If I decide to subscribe, I shall, from the beginning of the month following my
free parcel of books, receive six books each month for £5.94, post and packing free. If I decide not to subscribe I
shall write to you within 10 days. The free books are mine to keep in any case. I understand that I may cancel my
subscription at any time simply by writing to you. I am over 18 years of age.
Please write in BLOCK CAPITALS.

Name _____

Address _____

_____

_____ Postcode _____

SEND NO MONEY — TAKE NO RISKS

Remember postcodes speed delivery. Offer applies in U.K. only
and is not valid to present subscribers. Silhouette reserve the right
to exercise discretion in granting membership. If price changes
are necessary you will be notified.
Offer limited to one per household. Offer expires April 30th, 1986.

EP18SD